DARCY'S MIDSUMMER MADNESS

A PRIDE AND PREJUDICE VARIATION

CASS GRIX

Copyright 2017 Beverly Farr Giroux

This story is a work of fiction. Names, characters, places, and incidents are products of the author's imagination or are used fictitiously. Any resemblance to actual events, locales, or persons, living or dead, is entirely coincidental.

All rights reserved.

No part of this publication can be reproduced or transmitted in any form or by any means, electronic or mechanical without permission in writing from the author.

Cover design by beetifulbookcovers.com
Cover image by vaver/shutterstock.com

Website: www.cassgrix.com
　　Facebook: https://www.facebook.com/Cass-Grix-1271639419512755/
　　Email: mailto:cass.grix.author@gmail.com

1
SUNDAY

FITZWILLIAM DARCY

"Where is Mr. Darcy, Louisa?" Miss Bingley's shrill voice is unmistakeable. "Have you seen him?"

I sit silently with a volume of William Blake in my lap, hoping that my friend's sister will continue down the hall and not search for me in the library. I am sitting near one of the library windows in a tall, high-backed chair, out of sight from an opened door, but discoverable if Miss Bingley searches within.

I hold my breath, unwilling to call out to declare my presence, but also unwilling to hide behind the draperies like someone in a French farce, although I am sorely tempted to do so.

Not for the first time in the past month, I wish I were anywhere but at Netherfield Park, visiting Charles Bingley. I should never have agreed to visit him and to stay so long, but after my sister's near elopement in early June, I wanted to spend time with someone calm and rational. My fifteen-year-old sister Georgiana is presently at my estate in Derbyshire, being watched over by a new companion, Mrs. Annesley. Our parents are both dead and I am my sister's guardian, a duty I share with my Matlock cousin, Colonel Fitzwilliam.

Georgiana believes her heart has been broken and she spends her days crying, brooding, playing melancholy songs on the pianoforte and reading depressing poetry. I hope that a few weeks away from her mean-hearted brother – myself – and the beauty of Pemberley in the summer will have a beneficial effect.

I would have left Netherfield days earlier if I had not met and become intrigued by Miss Elizabeth Bennet.

And I would leave now, if it weren't for the deplorable weather – we have had several days of torrential rain - and for the upcoming ball. Bingley likes to tease me about not liking to dance and I do not want to look as if I am running away.

So I will stay for the ball which will be held Tuesday, two days from now, and then I will leave for London and Darcy House the following morning. After a week in Town, I will return to Pemberley. I will be there in time for the hunting at the end of August.

I hear Mrs. Hurst say, "I saw Mr. Darcy playing billiards with Charles."

That was an hour earlier, but fortunately Miss Bingley believes her sister and I hear their footsteps as they walk away from the closed library door.

I take a deep breath, thankful for the reprieve.

I did not realize until recently how irritating Miss Bingley can be. She often flirted with me in the past, but in a casual, half-hearted way that was almost amusing. She is a handsome young woman with Town manners and a sarcastic wit. Like me, she is quick to find fault with others. But during this visit, she has become more persistent in her attentions to me, no doubt as a response to my mad infatuation for Miss Elizabeth. I have tried to keep my admiration for that young woman hidden, but I spoke out of turn once or twice, betraying myself, and Miss Bingley pounced on my weakness like a cat on a mouse.

She likes to needle me, imagining Mrs. Bennet as my future mother-in-law.

But she does not say anything that I do not say to myself. I know it is foolishness to consider Miss Elizabeth Bennet as a potential bride.

Elizabeth Bennet is the second daughter of a local gentleman – a pretty girl of average height with curling hair and the most fascinating eyes I have ever seen. She is intelligent, she is pert, and she has a way of lifting her chin with a defiant air that makes me want to sweep her off her feet and carry her to Pemberley.

Not that I ever would. She is completely unsuitable to become the Mistress of Pemberley.

Her manners are too informal; her humour too mercurial.

And her family is atrocious. Her mother is vulgar, her sisters except for the eldest, named Jane, are all silly, ignorant girls. Lydia particularly. I have never seen such a loud, irreverent girl. She is always laughing and running about, heedless of those around her. How can anyone think that she is ready to be out in public? I shudder to think what Georgiana would do if she took Lydia as an example.

Miss Elizabeth's extended relations are no better. She has one uncle who lives in Meryton, a lawyer by profession, and another uncle in who lives in Cheapside, in Trade. Her father, although born a gentleman, has done nothing to improve himself or his estate. From what Bingley says, the man is rumored to spend most of the day in his library.

Considering the ill-bred behavior of his family, I cannot blame him. In truth, I am sympathetic to his plight. I am hiding in the library today to avoid Miss Bingley.

I know that my family and friends would never accept Elizabeth Bennet into their social circles and they will be horrified by my lack of judgment if I pursue her.

No, although she is delightful and enchanting, she is not for me.

I look out the window at the grey sky and damp grounds. If the weather were better, I would go riding or take a long walk.

But I fear that if I did, I would be tempted to go to Longbourn. I am like a compass, but instead of pointing North, I am inexplicably drawn toward Elizabeth Bennet.

I saw her last a few days ago in Meryton. She was walking with her sisters and some male relation. I had ridden with Bingley to enquire after Jane Bennet's health. When we entered the village, I saw them on the street and my heart seemed to beat in my throat. Elizabeth was beautiful as always but she was standing beside George Wickham, my enemy – the man who tried to ruin my sister.

I was shocked and had to turn away before my anger overcame me.

But now I regret the missed opportunity to speak with her.

It occurs to me that I am only remaining at Netherfield so I can dance with Miss Elizabeth Bennet.

2

MONDAY

CAROLINE BINGLEY

Mr. Darcy is avoiding me. Ever since the Bennet sisters spent a few days at Netherfield, he has behaved differently.

I don't know what to do.

Louisa says I am imagining things – that he likes me as much as he ever did.

But that is the problem. I am beginning to think that he never cared for me, that all our conversations were nothing more than politeness on his part. I fear that he never saw me as anything more than the sister of his friend.

On Monday morning, I sit calmly before a mirror while my lady's maid arranges my blonde hair into ringlets, but inwardly I am seething.

It is all Miss Elizabeth Bennet's fault. She has

bewitched Darcy with her fine eyes. What can he see in that blousy, plump girl? She isn't even pretty. She has almost no dowry and she can't speak Italian.

It is unfair. What was the point of my attending Mrs. Whitmore's School for Young Ladies and acquiring a score of accomplishments if it does not help me get the husband I want? I am twenty-three-years-old, almost an old maid. Louisa was already married when she was my age, and Charles is beginning to look at me with disappointment as if I will be living with him forever. I refused two proposals last year as I waited for Mr. Darcy to declare himself.

It is all so infuriating.

I have wanted to marry Mr. Darcy from the first moment I saw him. He is perfect for me: tall, dark and handsome with an income of ten thousand pounds a year. And his estate Pemberley in Derbyshire is just what I want.

So what am I to do? How am I to make him notice me?

Then I remember the rumours about Mrs. Wyatt. She is an older woman who lives in a small cottage outside Meryton. My lady's maid says she is a witch. I don't believe that, but I've heard whispers about her love potions.

After breakfast, I send the carriage for her.

Before luncheon, she is in my sitting room. Mrs. Wyatt is a tiny, wrinkled woman with shocking white hair underneath a neat cap. "Thank you for coming," I tell her and motion for her to be seated. "I hope the rain wasn't too troublesome."

"Oh, no, miss. I like the rain for it helps my gardens."

I say, "I've heard you have a talent with herbs."

"Yes, miss."

I see no benefit in wasting time with conversational niceties. I wait until the footman has left the room and then ask, "Can you make love potions?"

"I can, but they are very dangerous, miss."

"In what way?"

"It is best not to tamper with affairs of the heart, miss."

She reminds me of the merchants in London, pretending a scarcity to increase their prices. "Are you refusing to help me?"

"No, miss. I can make you a potion, but it will take time."

I do not have time, for Charles has discussed leaving for London after the Ball and I am afraid that Darcy will go with him, never to return.

"I need it tomorrow morning."

"That is not enough time."

"If it is a matter of money, I can pay double your usual price."

Mrs. Wyatt considers the matter, then says, "Very well, but I must warn you that since I do not have time for the herbs to steep for days, the potion will not last long. It may only last about twenty-four hours, possibly more or less."

Twenty-four hours should be sufficient if it results in a proposal. As a man of honour, Darcy would never go back on his word.

Mrs. Wyatt adds, "Also, the effect of the potion depends upon the intelligence and will of the recipient."

"I don't understand."

"Some individuals are less susceptible. Just as some people become inebriated after one glass of wine and others remain sober after drinking an entire bottle of wine."

That makes sense. "Very well," I say. "I want a bottle of your strongest love potion, with enough for a dozen doses." I want to be certain I have sufficient dosage to entrap Mr. Darcy, and I would prefer that the spell last until we have tied the knot.

Mrs. Wyatt's eyes grow wide. "I don't believe it is wise to have such a large amount. What if it got into the wrong hands?"

I reach into my reticule and withdraw several pound bank notes. "I will decide what is wise," I say firmly as I press the papers into her outstretched hand. "Now go and concoct your magic."

ELIZABETH BENNET

"Miss Elizabeth, may I speak with you for a moment?"

I turn to face my cousin, Mr. Collins. He is a tall, heavy set young man of five and twenty, neither handsome nor well-figured, and a recent guest at Longbourn, our home. Since our family has been blessed – my father might say cursed – with five daughters and no sons, Mr. Collins will one day inherit Longbourn according to the terms of the entail.

He is also a clergyman and in search of a wife. In the past few days, he has singled me out for his attentions and every day I fear that he will propose. "Yes," I say carefully, striving for civility but not encouragement. "You may speak with me."

He sits next to me on the settee. My mother, who is eager for all her daughters to marry, beams her approval. We are all of us – except my father who prefers the quiet of the library – sitting in the drawing room. My two youngest sisters Kitty and Lydia are playing cards, Mary is reading, while Jane and I have been sewing.

I scoot over several inches to one side so that Mr. Collin's thick thigh does not brush the thin muslin of my skirt. The thought of marrying him and being the recipient of his passions makes me want to vomit.

Mr. Collins clears his throat as if he is going to make an important announcement and I find myself staring at his large Adam's apple.

He says, "As you know, we have all been invited to Mr. Bingley's ball, and I hope, I pray, that you will honour me with the first two dances, Cousin Elizabeth."

My younger sister Kitty giggles and Lydia rolls her eyes at me as if to say, "Better you than I."

Two dances with Mr. Collins. The prospect is horrifying, for he is a prosy, irritating man and will no doubt prove to be an unbearable dance partner, but if I wish to dance at all tomorrow evening, I cannot refuse him. "As you wish," I say quietly.

He leans forward and whispers at me, his breath warm on my ear. "I wish for many things, Miss Elizabeth."

I shudder and lean backwards, giving Jane a panicked look to seek her assistance.

"Mr. Collins," she says cheerfully, walking over to interrupt us. "Have you seen our father's collection of sea shells?"

"I have not," he says politely. "But I am willing to have you show me."

"It is over here," Jane says and motions across the room. "On the wall."

At her prompting, Mr. Collins rises from the settee and walks across the room to join her. "I know nothing of seashells," he says. "But I am willing to learn."

Later that afternoon, as I go upstairs to dress for dinner, my mother pulls me aside. "Lizzy, I want you to be especially attentive to Mr. Collins tonight."

"I hope I will always be polite."

"I want you to be more than polite. Smile at him. Agree with what he says. Gentlemen like that."

Sometimes I wonder if that is how my mother caught my father's eye. He was a quiet, studious man and she had been a pretty, vivacious young woman. He married her in the blindness of passion, but time has lessened her appeal and now they rarely speak except for him to tease her and for her to complain.

My mother adds, "Remember that when your father dies, Mr. Collins can throw us out into the hedgerows if he wishes."

My mother often reminds us of that fact. She continues, "But if Jane marries Mr. Bingley and you marry Mr. Collins, we shall all be taken care of."

Mr. Bingley is our newest neighbour, a handsome, good-natured young man who is renting Netherfield Park, a home only three miles from Longbourn. He is rumoured to have a fortune of four thousand pounds a year, and he seems to like Jane. He and his sister Miss Bingley came to our home personally a few days before to invite us to their ball.

"Mr. Collins has not proposed to me," I say quietly. *And I hope that he never will.*

"Then I shall give him a few hints to spur him along."

"Please, Mama, I wish you would not. I don't want to marry Mr. Collins."

"Not want to marry?" she repeats, incredulous. "You are too foolish to know your own mind. He is perfectly suitable. And you won't find any better, for you have already ruined your chances with everyone else in Meryton. Men don't like bluestockings or outspoken women."

My mother thinks that any woman who reads more than the fashion magazines is a bluestocking, but there is no point in arguing with her. All I can hope is that Mr. Collins will decide that I am not to his taste. I wish he would transfer his affections to my sister Mary. She is of a serious mind and fancies herself to be a philosopher. She would make a much better wife for a clergyman than I would. And she is the only one of us five daughters who seems to like Mr. Collins' tedious conversation.

That evening after supper, Mr. Collins asks to play backgammon with me and both he and my mother are annoyed when I win. "You are a surprisingly good player, Cousin Elizabeth," Mr. Collins says, try to mask his irritation. "And I don't mind losing. No, one should never sit down at a backgammon table if one is not prepared to lose. My patroness Lady Catherine de Bourgh is an excellent backgammon player, as well." He smirks at me and gives a little bow of deference that I assume he thinks is complimentary. "I hope one day, Cousin Elizabeth that you will have an opportunity to play with her. Although, I trust that your respect for her will curb your competitive nature."

Mr. Collins often talks about Lady Catherine de Bourgh and her daughter Anne de Bourgh. Lady Catherine seems to be a strong willed, opinionated woman.

"Does Lady Catherine always win when she plays you, Mr. Collins?" my father asks slyly.

"I consider it my duty," Mr. Collins says. "To provide entertainment and sport without directly challenging her."

"So, it is your duty to lose?" I ask.

"Yes, for she prefers it."

"Quite sensible, I am sure," my mother murmurs and glares at me.

I begin to count the minutes until bedtime.

Later, I speak to Jane about it in our bedroom as we prepare for sleep. She unfastens my dress in the back and holds it while I step out. I ask, "What am I supposed to do – let Mr. Collins win?"

Jane says, "The right gentlemen for you won't mind if you win."

"Precisely," I say and hang up my gown in our closet. I change into a loose night rail and sit down on the bed that we share. I watch as Jane, already dressed for bed, brushes her long blonde hair. She is the true beauty of the family. "If you do marry Mr. Bingley," I say, "Let me come live with you. I will mend all your clothes and care for your children as a favourite aunt."

Jane blushes. "Mr. Bingley is a most excellent gentleman, but he has not said anything to me to imply that he wishes to marry me."

Jane is too humble. I say, "For once, I agree with our mother. I think he is madly in love with you and that he will propose any minute now."

Jane smiles shyly. "Do you think so?"

"I know so. I have never seen a man so besotted in my life. The way he watches you – as if you are an angel."

Jane says, "The way Mr. Darcy looks at you?"

Mr. Darcy is Mr. Bingley's wealthy friend. When I first saw him at the Meryton Assembly, I was favourably impressed. He was tall and handsome with a noble mien. But within a few minutes, it was clear that he was proud and conceited. He looked down on everyone, considering himself above his company. He refused to dance with me and I have disliked him ever since.

My dislike was strengthened when I learned that

he had injured Mr. Wickham, a new handsome soldier in town. Mr. Darcy denied Wickham a living that Darcy Senior had promised, thereby ruining Mr. Wickham's prospects.

I laugh at Jane's suggestion. "Nonsense. You know what he said when we first met. *She is tolerable, I suppose, but not handsome enough to tempt me.*"

"He must have changed his mind, for I saw the way he looked at you when we were both at Netherfield."

A week ago, we had both been at Netherfield. Jane had gone to dinner with Miss Bingley and Mrs. Hurst and caught a cold. She spent several days at Netherfield, recovering, and I visited for four days to care for her. During that time, I ate dinner and spent several evenings in Mr. Darcy's presence. I found him proud, vain, and arrogant - just as he had been before. I wonder how he and Mr. Bingley who is always a gentleman can stand to be friends.

Jane says, "I think you have as much a chance of receiving a proposal as I do – perhaps even greater."

"Not from Mr. Darcy," I argue. "The only proposal on my horizon is one from Mr. Collins."

Jane nods. "What are you going to say if he proposes?"

"No, naturally, but I am hoping to discourage him so he never asks."

Jane sighs. "That would be kinder. The poor man. I hope his heart won't be broken."

"His heart? How can his heart be affected?" I protest. "He has known me less than two weeks. And even if his heart were broken, surely you don't want me to marry him only out of politeness?"

"No, but I still feel sorry for him."

"You are too kind."

"I just wish there was someone for everyone."

"Now you sound like our mother."

"I just want everyone to be happy."

Dear Jane. She is too good. I often feel like a cynical shrew in comparison to her goodness. I ask, "Do you think Mr. Collins might like Mary instead?"

3

TUESDAY, MORNING

JAMES PUCK

I sit in the kitchen, awaiting orders. As a footman, I usually assist with meals, but since the Bingleys are hosting a ball today, there are many extra tasks. Miss Bingley calls me into the sitting room. She's a handsome woman, but a little too thin for my taste. Sometimes when I am in the same room with her, I entertain myself by imagining what she looks like without her shift. She says, "I will make this quick. I have heard that you have been bothering the maids."

I smirk. "No one has complained, yet."

"That is beside the point," she says sharply. "One of the scullery maids is with child and I have had to dismiss her."

Poor Ginny. I liked her and I will miss her, but

she knew the risks. I didn't force her, and I wasn't her first lover, either. A man can't be blamed for taking what's offered, can he?

Miss Bingley continues to speak. "And I will have to dismiss you as well."

I have heard this before. I mentally swear, but keep my face expressionless. "Today? But won't you need all your help for the Ball?"

Miss Bingley considers my words and says, "Very well. You may stay until after tomorrow when the house has been set back to rights after the ball."

A reprieve. "Yes, ma'am. Thank you, ma'am," I say politely and give her my best subservient smile. With luck, after the ball, she might forget that she wants to sack me.

Miss Bingley frowns as she looks at me. "Mrs. Bailey says you have a rebellious attitude."

Mrs. Bailey is an old cow. But from experience I know that if the housekeeper is against me, there is no chance I will be able to stay at Netherfield.

Miss Bingley adds, "I am only keeping you on because you are tall and look good in the uniform."

Hey ho, I wonder and look at her closely. Does Miss Bingley fancy a little tickle and pinch? She doesn't seem the type, but I've heard tales from other footmen at other households.

But then she finishes our conversation with a

brisk, "Perform your duties well tonight, and I will provide a good written character. Otherwise, not."

Later, I sit in the kitchen again, nursing my wounded pride. Miss Bingley is a shrew, a dried up old maid. She thinks she will marry her brother's rich friend, but she won't. Why would Mr. Darcy take that bitter stick when he could have a warm armful like Miss Elizabeth?

Ah, Miss Elizabeth, I think. Now there's a pretty girl. I like Miss Elizabeth because she smiles and always looks like she's ready to laugh. I do not blame Mr. Darcy for preferring her over Miss Bingley at all. Of course, she doesn't have much dowry, but Darcy doesn't need that. He's as rich as Croesus.

I spend half an hour imagining what I would do if I had Darcy's fortune.

Then Tom, one of the other footmen, walks by me. "Have you bought your time, yet?"

I shake my head. "No. Are they dividing up the days now?" There's a wager among the servants as to when Mr. Bingley will propose to Miss Bennet, Miss Elizabeth's older sister Jane. There is also some talk about when Mr. Darcy will propose to Miss Elizabeth, but I don't think that prospect is as likely. Miss Elizabeth seems the kind of feisty girl who might slap a man if she thinks him impertinent.

What I would not give to see that.

I smile, remembering the day she first came to

Netherfield. Her sister was sick and she walked all the way, arriving at breakfast. I was standing in the breakfast room when she arrived. Footmen are trained to stand without expression, but that does not mean we don't pay attention.

Later Barney, the other footman on duty that day, said she looked like one of those paintings. "You know, the shepherdesses with their hair all blown about."

I agreed. And I could also well imagine her like one of the naked goddesses on the ceiling in the dining room.

Miss Elizabeth is my kind of beauty. Not too skinny, not too plump.

A knock at the kitchen door interrupts my thoughts. I answer the door. It's Ned from the village. Poor bastard. He is drenched from the rain. He's fifty if he's a day and he still runs errands. When I'm his age, I plan to have a little shop, selling snuff. I'll be my own man. Ned holds a dark glass bottle with cork in the top in a death grip. When I offer to take it from him, he says, "It's from Mrs. Wyatt for Miss Bingley. I'm supposed to hand it to her directly, with this letter."

Mrs. Wyatt, eh? That is interesting. I wonder what Miss Bingley wants from that old witch.

Ned sneezes.

"I'll take it to her," I offer. "I promise. Why don't you sit down and have a cup of tea before you go?"

"I'd like that," he says and looks at the fireplace longingly.

I leave, like I'm pretending to take the bottle upstairs to Miss Bingley, but instead, I hide it in a cupboard. After Ned leaves, I take a hot knife and carefully remove the wax seal on the letter so I can read it. Mrs. Wyatt wrote:

Remember that the love potion only has limited effectiveness and act accordingly. No more than one teaspoon per dose.

I whistle. A love potion? How marvelous. I suppose that Miss Bingley wants to douse Mr. Darcy's wine. That should be amusing.

I don't like Mr. Darcy. He's too high in the instep for me, but I don't hate him. If I had his face and fortune, I'd be twice as proud and half as pleasant as he is now.

His valet Bowles says he's a fair man.

I replace the wax and consider taking it upstairs to Miss Bingley. She should tip me extra for bringing her the letter and keeping the matter confidential.

Then I reconsider. Why should I be loyal to her?

Miss Bingley is dismissing me after all. Why should I not have a little fun before I go?

Back in the kitchen, I see a tray of pastries in the pantry. I taste one, savoring the buttery pastry and the sweet fig filling, then I arrange the remaining pastries so that no one will know that I ate one. Then, in a moment of genius, I decide to dribble some of the love potion upon each pastry.

The dark liquid seeps into the dark fig filling and is completely hidden.

I laugh, imagining the chaos that could ensue.

When the bottle is empty, I piss into it and add some crumbled herbs to make it look legitimate, and then take it and the letter upstairs to Miss Bingley.

I don't know if the potion will work, but if it does, Netherfield Ball will be a ball never to be forgotten.

MR. COLLINS

I sit in the siting room at Longbourn, imagining how pleasant it will be when Mr. Bennet dies and I inherit his home. Not that I expect him to die any time soon, for unfortunately he seems to be of excellent health, but I will enjoy owning such a neat, well-designed home. I am already making plans of the changes I will make to the gardens.

Miss Mary plays the pianoforte while I pretend

to read and the other Bennet daughters talk about rosebuds for their shoes.

I don't know what Lady Catherine would think of rosebuds for dancing shoes. Miss Anne de Bourgh has never wore rosebuds, but then again, she has never been well enough to dance.

I glance at the beautiful Miss Bennet who is hemming a shirt. When I first came to Longbourn I had hoped that she, as the eldest, would be my bride. But Mrs. Bennet informed me that she was soon to be engaged, so I shifted my attentions to Miss Elizabeth. Miss Elizabeth is not as beautiful as her older sister Jane, but she is still very pretty. Unfortunately, she does not have the calm serenity of Miss Bennet. There is something too lively and disconcerting in her eyes. But I am convinced that once she is my wife, under the tutelage of Lady Catherine, she will learn to moderate her vivacity.

I imagine how pleased Lady Catherine will be when I bring Miss Elizabeth to Rosing's Park as my wife. The Saturday night before I left Hunsford, she was specific in her instructions. "Mr. Collins," she says. "You must marry. A clergyman like you must marry. Choose properly, choose a gentlewoman for my sake, and for your own, let her be an active, useful sort of person, not brought up high, but able to make a small income go a good way."

Lady Catherine always gives excellent advice.

She added, "Find such a woman as soon as you can, bring her to Hunsford, and I will visit her."

With her advice in mind, I decided that I would marry one of my cousins. How convenient to have five eligible young women to choose from. Now that I am here, though, I realize that I would never consider either of the youngest two: Catherine – her sisters all call her Kitty, which I think is foolishness – or Lydia. Catherine giggles too much, and Lydia is much too young to be out in public. She laughs too loud and doesn't have an ounce of decorum. I have tried to give some advice to Mrs. Bennet on how to curb her younger daughters, but she only smiles and says, "I daresay you are right, Mr. Collins, but young girls are not all as wise as you."

I watch Miss Elizabeth, thinking of how I will enjoy being married to her. She will make a pleasant armful. I have been celibate all my life, but I am eager to start a family.

I am certain Lady Catherine will advise me on how many children I should have.

4

TUESDAY, MIDDAY

CAROLINE BINGLEY

The love potion smells foul, but I manage to put a tablespoon full in Darcy's soup at our luncheon. I watch his every mouthful and am alarmed as he takes only two spoonfuls and then refuses to eat the rest. "Are you not hungry?" I ask. "Onion Soup is one of your favourites, I thought."

Darcy says, "I am not very hungry."

Charles says, "It is good not to eat too much. I am planning to save room for all the desserts at the Ball tonight. Caroline, did you arrange for Cook to make my favourite pastries?"

"Yes, Charles. There will be a vast assortment of apple, apricot, mincemeat and fig pastries."

"Fig is the best," Charles says.

Darcy teases him. "You have such a sweet tooth.

If you don't curb yourself, you will end up as large as Sir William Lucas."

Later, before tea, I privately take one of the tea cakes and make a small indentation in its base with a spoon, then pour the golden love potion into it. Then when the servants bring the other cakes, I add my doctored cake to theirs. I wait, watching Mr. Darcy's every move, and when I think the time is right, I place that exact cake on a plate for him.

"Do try the tea cakes," I tell him with a smile. "I ordered them especially for you."

FITZWILLIAM DARCY

At tea time, the food tastes terrible, even the tea cakes. Miss Bingley, noticing my distaste says with concern, "What is the matter, Mr. Darcy?"

"I am sorry. I think I may be coming down with a cold. Nothing tastes right today."

Bingley takes a large bite of his cake. "Mine is fine. I wonder if your illness is merely a ploy to keep from having to attend the ball tonight?"

"No, I am actually looking forward to it."

Miss Bingley says quickly, "If you are not feeling well, I can have Cook prepare a tisane for you to drink. She is a wonder at making restorative drinks."

Bingley says, "Do drink it, Darcy. I don't want you to be under the weather tonight."

"I will go speak to Cook, right away," Miss Bingley says and hurries from the room, her long muslin day dress fluttering behind her as she walks briskly.

Bingley sniffs my half-eaten tea cake. "That is a bit off," he agrees.

Mr. Hurst, who had been napping, rouses himself sufficiently to enquire, "Eh. What is off?"

"Tea cakes," Mrs. Hurst says.

"Then don't eat them," he says practically.

"I won't," I promise.

After a few minutes, Bingley has had his fill of tea cakes, bread and jam. "Come walk with me," he says and together we step outside into the Netherfield gardens. There are stone walks, statues and sculpted shrubberies. The air is clean and fresh after the days of near constant rain. The ground is damp, however, and soon the bottom few inches of our boots are covered with dirt and bits of grass.

Bingley points out where there will be lanterns tonight. "The weather is fine enough that some people might want to go outside. I may even have a harpist set up out of doors on the balcony."

That seems excessive to me, but it is his party.

"And the fireworks are to be set up on that hill, past that tree there. Everyone should be able to see them from the ballroom." The ballroom at Netherfield has a wall of floor to ceiling windows.

I can see the wood scaffolding and there are several servants on a platform. They will assist Signor Invetto who has been hired to supervise the display. Bingley has always been fascinated by fireworks, and he has dragged me to numerous displays over the years. I am just grateful that he has hired a professional so he does not blow his head off or set Netherfield on fire. "This will be a night to remember," I say finally.

Bingley beams. "I want everything to be just right. But now that we are alone, I must talk to you about Jane Bennet. Do you think she likes me?"

"I think everyone likes you, Charles." Bingley has such an open, friendly nature. It is impossible not to like him. He is one of my closest friends, completely loyal and kind.

"No, I mean, do you think she likes me enough to marry me?"

I had noted Bingley's interest in Miss Bennet earlier, but I did not think it had risen to this level. "I don't know," I say finally. "She is a very calm woman." Jane was tepid when compared to her more vibrant sister Elizabeth. "Frankly, I don't know if Miss Bennet is capable of loving anyone."

"I disagree. When we are together, she enjoys my company."

"Then it is up to you to decide. Don't ask my opinion if you don't want to hear it."

"No, I do want your opinion," he persists.

"Then it is this. If you ask Jane Bennet to marry you, she will say yes. Her mother wants her to marry a wealthy man, and you meet those requirements. Whether Jane Bennet has any tender feelings for you, remains to be seen. Personally, I would not want to be married for my fortune. I want a woman who loves me passionately."

Bingley says, "Do you think I should speak to her father first?"

I realize that he is not listening to half the words I say. "What, right now?"

"No, tonight at the ball."

I shake my head at his impetuosity. "No, it will be too noisy and it would be difficult to speak to him privately. I think it would be much better to wait at least until tomorrow morning."

"I will," Bingley says. "Or I will wait a week until I come back from my trip to London. I think that is it. I will buy a ring in London."

"I think it is better to wait," I tell him. "As lovely as Jane Bennet is, you do not know her well." It is what I tell myself about Elizabeth Bennet. It is madness for me to consider marriage with her.

"But I have never loved a young woman as much as I love her. She is the most beautiful girl I have ever met."

"Do you love Miss Bennet because of her beauty or because of her character?"

"Both, of course."

"Beauty will fade," I remind. "And ten years from now, she will look like her mother."

"I think Mrs. Bennet is a handsome woman."

I feel like throwing up my hands in despair. The man is completely besotted. "Do what you wish, but remember that fools rush in where angels fear to tread."

"Miss Bennet is an angel," he says.

Later that afternoon, as I prepare for the ball, a footman brings me a tisane. "With Miss Bingley's compliments, sir."

I smell the nasty concoction. It smells like a barnyard. There is no way I will drink it. I hand the drink to Bowles, my valet. "Get rid of this."

"Yes, sir."

LYDIA BENNET

I look out the sitting room window, drumming my fingers on the windowpane. It is raining again. It is so boring. But then John returns from town with our shoe roses. I choose the best pair and Mary says she does not want hers. Jane offers to sew them on for her, if she wishes, but Mary still declines.

"You can sew mine," I say, and hand them to Jane. "Your stitches are so much nicer than mine."

Lizzy says quietly, "That is because you have no patience."

I stick my tongue out at her when Mama is not looking.

Lizzy is my least favourite sister, always thinking she knows best. Mary is a bore, quoting her books, but Lizzy is so bossy.

And worst of all, she hogs Mr. Wickham's attention every time we are in the same company. Mr. Wickham is the newest officer in the regiment, and the handsomest man in the world. He has a way of looking at me from the sides of his eyes that gives me delightful shivers. I can just imagine what a good kisser he will be. Much better than William Cole, I am sure.

I look at my sisters with smug satisfaction, knowing that I have been kissed twice already and they have never been kissed at all.

Mr. Wickham will be my next conquest, as long as I can keep him away from Lizzy.

She flirts with him outrageously, and he is too much of a gentleman to ignore her. But tonight I intend to dance with him before she does, for Elizabeth is engaged to dance the first two dances with our cousin Mr. Collins. I nearly crowed with joy when I heard of it. I would rather die than marry

Mr. Collins, but I think Lizzy will suit him admirably, and once she is engaged, I will have Mr. Wickham all to myself.

And after I dance with Mr. Wickham tonight I am going to lead him to the card tables, so I can spend even more time with him.

There is nothing I like better than a Ball, and I believe I should take some credit for the event, because I am the one who reminded Mr. Bingley of his duty when we all went to visit Jane when she was ill. If I had not reminded him, he might not have given the ball at all.

I hope when Jane marries Bingley that they will give a ball every month.

5

TUESDAY, EVENING

MARY BENNET

I sit in the carriage on the way to the Netherfield Ball, crushed between Jane and Kitty. There are so many of us tonight that we are travelling in two vehicles. My father and Mr. Collins, who do not have ballgowns that could be ruined by rain, follow behind us in the curricle.

I hold my gloved hands neatly in my lap and wonder how I will endure the evening. I hate balls. I am not like Kitty and Lydia. I don't mind dancing, but I am not good at it. And as the plainest of five Bennet sisters, I am often overlooked. I never know what to say and when I quote one of the books I have been reading, no one listens.

I look over at Jane who is beautiful and sweet. I don't envy her beauty because she is so good, but I wonder if Jane will marry Mr. Bingley. He seems like a very nice man. Nicer than our father who makes too many jokes.

I don't think I will ever marry, but if I do, I would like a man like Mr. Bingley for he is handsome and kind and has a large house.

But I would not like to live next door to my mother.

I wonder if Mr. Bingley has any unmarried cousins.

I glance briefly at my mother who is smiling and humming to herself. As we near Netherfield, she says, "Oh Jane, just look at all the lanterns."

I fear that I will be an old maid forever. That no one will want me, and I will be forced to care for my mother and father until they die.

The only thing that gives me joy is to read and play the pianoforte. It is my only talent.

Perhaps I will be able to play a song or two tonight.

MRS. BENNET

I have never seen a more beautiful sight than Netherfield all lit up with lanterns. And so many handsome footmen in liveried coats. It makes my heart flutter to think that one day all of this will belong to Jane. Jane is so beautiful tonight, with her hair styled high and her new blue gown. As we enter the main entrance hall, I see the Lucases and greet them. I pity Lady Lucas who has such a plain daughter. Even my Mary is prettier. I see that Charlotte also has a new dress – green with gold lace that does nothing for her complexion. The gown was a shocking expense, but I suppose Lady Lucas thinks she must spend money to make anyone notice Charlotte at all.

Poor child. It is not Charlotte's fault that she is so plain, but she compounds the matter by refusing to flirt.

No one is ever going to marry her.

And then we are before Mr. Bingley and his sisters, greeting them. Miss Bingley wears an elaborate headdress with ostrich feathers, quite impressive. I say, "Oh, Mr. Bingley, it is so wonderful to see you."

Mr. Bingley bows slightly. "Thank you for coming. Mr. Bennet, Mrs. Bennet. I hope you will enjoy the dancing." I watch how he beams at Jane.

"I hope you will honor me with the first dance," he asks Jane.

Jane blushes and agrees.

I turn to Mr. Bennet and raise my eyebrows meaningfully as if to say *See, they will be married by Michaelmas.*

Mr. Bennet shakes his head. "Do not count your

chickens, Mrs. Bennet," he says and then adds in a whisper, "Or your sons-in-law."

I glare at him. I wish Mr. Bennet would not be so pessimistic.

LYDIA BENNET

I can't believe it. Mr. Wickham is not here. I corner Mr. Denny as soon as I can to ask him where Mr. Wickham is. He says Wickham was called away by business to go to Town.

I am so angry I can hardly see straight. I have planned to dance with Wickham for days and I have new rosebuds on my dancing slippers.

There is no choice but to drown my sorrows by finding something tasty at the refreshment tables.

I drink two glasses of wine, eat several pastries and I think I like the fig ones best, but one of them has a bitter taste, so I drink another cup of punch to wash down the taste in my mouth.

I look around the room and see that Mr. Darcy is standing over by one wall, by himself. Hateful man. I know that he is the reason Wickham chose not to attend the ball. The wine has given me courage, so I decide I will give that haughty gentleman a piece of my mind. How dare he treat Wickham so unfairly?

Wickham should have been a clergyman and I think he would have made an excellent one. I think if a man is going to give sermons, he should be handsome so that young women like me can enjoy themselves in church.

But as I walk over to Mr. Darcy I realize that he is twice as handsome as Wickham. Why did I never notice that before?

He has thick dark hair curling back from his forehead and the most piercingly blue eyes. His shoulders are wide and he looks so fit in his tightly tailored coat.

I realize that half of Wickham's charm came from his uniform. Mr. Darcy does not need that artifice. He is beautiful without a redcoat.

ELIZABETH BENNET

I look around the Netherfield Ballroom, looking for Mr. Wickham, but I cannot see him. Mr. Denny tells me that Wickham had business in town. I believe that Wickham has chosen to stay away to avoid Mr. Darcy. Wickham has told me how Darcy ruined his prosects by denying him a living that Darcy's father had promised him.

I seek out Charlotte Lucas to commiserate with her.

"Hello, Miss Eliza," she says, as I approach.

I look around the room.

"Whom are you looking for?" she asks.

I shake my head. "No one, really. Since Mr. Wickham is not here, there is no one interesting." I briefly see Mr. Darcy glaring at me. Odious man.

"What of your cousin, Mr. Collins?" Charlotte asks.

I roll my eyes as my answer.

Charlotte says, "Why do you dislike him so?"

"I would like him well enough if my mother did not want me to marry him."

Charlotte says, "He is going to inherit Longbourn."

"Please let us talk of something else," I tell her.

She suggests that we both walk over to the food tables. "Oh, look at the pastries," she says and takes one. "Don't you want one?"

I lift one up to my nose and sniff it. "No, it is fig." I shudder and place the pastry back down on the tray. "I don't like figs. But here is an apple one." I eat that instead. From my visit two weeks ago, I know that Netherfield has an excellent cook.

Charlotte takes a bite of her fig pastry and frowns slightly. "It is a little bitter," she explains. "My mother's figs are much better." She looks around as if looking for a place to return the half-eaten pastry to the tray, then decides to finish it.

At this moment, Mr. Collins comes to claim his dances.

"Miss Elizabeth," he says with a bow. "I believe

you have agreed to the first two dances?" He smiles in greeting to Charlotte. "Miss Lucas," he says formally and gives her a little bow as well.

"Mr. Collins," she says in return, her eyes wide. She curtsies and smiles at him and as I take his arm to go onto the dance floor she whispers to me, "Be kind to him."

FITZWILLIAM DARCY

I stand near a wall in the ballroom by myself. Bingley is busy with his duties as host, so I cannot speak with him and the only other person I wish to converse with is Elizabeth Bennet. She is speaking with her friend Miss Lucas and then is led off to the dance floor by her cousin Mr. Collins. I am not acquainted with Mr. Collins. I only know his name because I heard as he was being introduced to another. I watch as the musicians start the dance music.

If I cannot dance with Elizabeth myself, I will enjoy watching her as she dances with others.

She is beautiful tonight in a white gown with flower ribbons at the neck. Her dark curls are styled back away from her face with one lovely ringlet lying against a creamy shoulder. Her white gloves encase her slim arms and are fastened above her elbows. As she dances, the thin fabric of her gown sways and in the warm glow of candlelight, I see the occasional curve of waist and hip.

Unfortunately, Mr. Collins is an atrocious dancer, often stepping wrong and apologizing loudly. If it would not make matters worse, I would interrupt them and forcibly take his place. I long to dance with Elizabeth and wish that the German waltz were popular here.

"Lovely music, don't you agree?" a young woman asks.

I look down and to my surprise, it is Elizabeth's youngest sister, Lydia Bennet, who has never spoken a word to me before. I wonder why she is accosting me now.

The music is adequate, but nothing out of the ordinary, so I say nothing.

"Do you care to dance, Mr. Darcy?" she says.

What a forward chit. But I choose to consider her question hypothetical rather than specific. "In general, no, I do not care to dance." I say coolly in tones that have discouraged dozens of young women before. Hopefully she will leave and find another man to pester.

She pouts. "What is the point of attending a ball if you do not plan to dance?" she asks.

She is persistent. A less confident young woman would have left by now. "If you wish to dance, I am certain you can find other gentlemen who will accommodate you." I motion towards a group of soldiers across the room. "Perhaps a redcoat?"

She steps closer and looks up at me, batting her eyelashes. "I have no interest in redcoats when Mr. Darcy is present."

I can't believe that she is flirting with me. I step back in revulsion and find myself against the wall. "Excuse me," I say and sidestep away from her to make my escape.

"If you do not wish to dance, would you like to play cards?" she calls after me.

I walk away from her as quickly as I can.

LYDIA BENNET

Mr. Darcy does not want to dance with me, but I am not discouraged. I love him. I can't believe that I ever considered Mr. Wickham, when Wickham is nothing to him. Ten thousand pounds a year. What a lark it will be, when I marry him and become Mistress of Pemberley. I am the youngest of my sisters, but I am determined to be the first to marry. Somehow, I will find a way to impress Mr. Darcy tonight.

I drink another glass of wine and plan.

6

TUESDAY, EVENING

ELIZABETH BENNET

Mr. Collins is a poor dancer, often taking the wrong steps. I am mortified.

After the two dances, I return to Charlotte. "Never again," I vow. "Remind me to never dance with that man again."

"Why not?" she asks.

"Did you not see what a bumbling fool he is? He kept stepping on my toes."

"He may not know all the steps, but that is no reason to complain," Charlotte says. "He showed you great honor by seeking you out as his first partner."

I frown. "You sound as if you like him."

"I don't know him well," Charlotte says practically. "But I do think he is a fine figure of a man."

I begin to think that my friend Charlotte may need spectacles. "Are you teasing me?"

"No, not at all. He is not as tall as Mr. Darcy or as amiable as Mr. Bingley, but there is something sweet and appealing about him."

I laugh. "You are teasing me."

"No, I am not. I did not particularly like him before, but tonight I feel as if I should amend my opinion."

I am astonished. At that moment, Mr. Darcy approaches and offers his hand. "Would you care to dance?"

In my state of mental confusion, I agree. "I will," I say and before I know it, we are both on the dance floor, taking our place in the set. I look around and see that many of my neighbours are surprised to see me dancing with Mr. Darcy. And Lydia is glaring at me as if she would like to stab me in the back. I know she is often annoyed by me, as I am often annoyed by her, but the intensity of her sudden anger is disconcerting. Normally at a ball, she would be dancing and not standing on the sides of the room, watching me.

"Are you all right?" Mr. Darcy asks.

We take the beginning steps and his gloved hands briefly touch mine. "I don't know," I say. "I am merely startled by some people's behavior tonight." Lydia and Charlotte are both acting strangely.

"Which persons?"

I look at him directly. "You are one."

This surprises him. He did not expect me to be so blunt. He says, "Why? What have I done that has surprised you?"

"I never thought that you would ask me to dance."

"I asked you to dance the other day when we were with Sir William Lucas."

"Yes, but that was only because he forced your hand."

"Believe me, Miss Bennet," Mr. Darcy says stiffly. "No one forces my hand."

I raise one eyebrow in disbelief. "Then I must find you capricious, sir."

He frowns as the steps of the dance separate us. When we are together again, he asks, "I pride myself on my constancy. In what way am I variable?"

"At the Meryton Assembly, I overheard you tell your friend Mr. Bingley that you did not wish to dance with me. You said that I was tolerable, but not handsome enough to tempt you."

Darcy draws his breath in sharply. "That was inexcusable."

He is embarrassed. For once I have humbled him, and it is a heady feeling. We separate again, turning with other partners, then come back together. His face is pale. He says, "I spoke in a fit of pique. I was annoyed with Bingley at the time and I was unkind to you. Can you forgive me?"

He sounds sincere, which alarms me even more than his prior insult. I have considered Mr. Darcy to be proud, arrogant and incapable of reform for weeks. "The dance floor is not the place for such a serious conversation, sir," I tell him. "But if it makes you feel better, your insult was more amusing than offensive, so I was not harmed."

His dark brows lower as if he is trying to determine my meaning. "I slighted your looks before, but now I consider you one of the handsomest women of my acquaintance."

"Ah, much better, Mr. Darcy," I tease. "Flattery is completely appropriate for the dance floor."

"I do not flatter," he says. "I try always to tell the truth."

I smile. "How uncomfortable for all your acquaintances. I believe a certain amount of dissembling is required in polite society. Otherwise we would all come to blows."

He smiles as well. "You are correct. But that is where silence comes in. Sometimes I choose not to speak to avoid offense, but when I do speak, I strive for complete honesty."

I cannot fault him for that sentiment. If true, it is an admirable trait. For the next several minutes we are both quiet as we continue with the dance.

But eventually the silence makes me brave. I decide to test his veracity. By our proximity, Mr. Darcy is forced to attend to my conversation, so I say, "When you saw me last, I was forming a new acquaintance. Perhaps you know him – Mr. George Wickham?"

Darcy's face is now as red as it was pale before as a deeper shade of hauteur overspreads his features. "I know him," he says stiffly.

I wait for further comment, and finally he speaks again. "Mr. Wickham is blessed with such happy manners that he makes friends easily. Unfortunately, he is less capable of retaining them."

"He has lost your friendship, that is clear."

Darcy's jaw tightens. "What lies has he told you?"

"Lies?" I counter. "Is it a lie that you refused to honor your father's final wishes? That you denied him a living that was in your power to bestow?"

"Miss Bennet," Darcy says sharply. "It is obvious to me that you take an eager interest in that man's fortunes, but you are correct that the ballroom is not a place for serious conversation. If you wish to know the truth of those matters, I will tell you. Normally, I do not wish to lay my private actions open to the world for their review or censure, but I wish to be honest with you."

Good heavens. I feel as if I have stirred up a hornet's nest. I have never seen Mr. Darcy so intense. "You do not need to tell me your secrets, sir."

He smiles wryly. "Rest assured, I will not tell you all my secrets. Only those involving Mr. Wickham."

I blink, astonished. Is Mr. Darcy flirting with me?

What magical change is this? Is everyone different tonight?

If I did not know better, I would think the ball was a dream. In dreams, people we know often act strangely.

But the music, the other dancers, and Darcy's hand on my hand are all real.

As the dance ends, we both walk to a corner of the ballroom, where there are some empty chairs and by mutual consent, we sit.

Darcy says, "It is true that I refused to give Wickham a living that my father intended for him when it became available, but that was because Wickham had previously given it up."

"I don't understand."

"I will start at the beginning," Darcy says. "George Wickham was the son of my father's steward. His father was a good man and my father greatly relied upon him. Wickham spent his youth at Pemberley and was often my companion. My father favoured him and supported him at school and afterwards at Cambridge. In his will, my father left Wickham a legacy of one thousand pounds and a bequest that he be given a profitable living once it was available."

I nod. All this Wickham told me himself at our second meeting.

Darcy continues, "My father had the highest opinion of Wickham. He saw only his engaging manners and quick wit. He did not know him as I knew him. We were of nearly the same age, and I saw him in unguarded moments. Wickham could not hide from me his immoral and corrupt propensities, his complete want of principle."

"You astonish me, sir. Are you saying that Wickham is a villain?"

Darcy's eyes grow dark. "He was definitely a villain to one I love best, but I will explain our history first. Wickham often cheats and lies, doing whatever he wishes with no regard for others, and he is only circumspect to keep from being discovered. He takes advantage of women and runs up debts. When my father died, we both agreed that he should not be a clergyman, so he requested a payment in lieu of the position and was given three thousand pounds in exchange."

"So much?"

Darcy nods. "He had some intention of studying the law, but it is more likely that he wasted it in profligate living."

I find this difficult to believe. How could

Wickham be so bad? But Darcy speaks so matter-of-factly. I wait to hear more of their history and the evil Wickham did to the woman Darcy loved.

Darcy says, "I did not hear from Wickham for three years, but then when the incumbent of the living died, Wickham approached me. Apparently the study of law had been unprofitable and he was now resolved on being ordained."

"He wanted the living."

"Yes, but I refused and his resentment was extreme. Our paths did not pass again until this summer, almost two months ago."

At this, Darcy stares out at the dancers on the ballroom floor. I see a muscle in his jaw tighten as he strives to contain his emotions. "Forgive me," he says finally, his voice husky. "This part of the tale is still very painful."

I wait, holding my breath.

"My sister Georgiana, my dearest sister, is only fifteen years old. She has been going to school in London and this spring, she took a journey to Ramsgate with the headmistress, a young woman named Mrs. Younge. She appeared capable and principled. I had no way of knowing it, but Mrs. Younge was in collusion with Wickham."

"Oh no," I whisper. "What happened?"

"Wickham joined them in Ramsgate and with Mrs. Younge's assistance, he courted Georgiana, persuading her to fall in love with him and to agree to an elopement." Darcy's voice lowered. "And he would have succeeded if I had not visited by chance a day or two before the intended elopement."

"Thank goodness."

"Yes, I know that I was fortunate. I visited unannounced to surprise Georgiana, and she told me all of it. She thought I would be happy for her and that I would give my blessing as soon as I knew how much she loved Wickham."

"Your poor sister."

"Yes. You can imagine how I responded. Mrs. Younge was dismissed and I took Georgiana back to Pemberley. I would have gladly challenged Wickham to a duel, but I did not want the scandal. Since then, it appears that he joined the army here at Meryton."

No wonder he looked at Wickham as if he would like to kill him when they met again.

Darcy added, "Wickham's chief object with my sister was unquestionably my sister's fortune which is thirty thousand pounds, but I also know that he wanted revenge upon me. If he had succeeded with Georgiana, his revenge would have been complete."

I nod, but my mind is in a turmoil. For a week, seven short days, I have thought Wickham to be everything good, but I realize that I was foolish to accept his statements so completely. What did I know of him other than his flattery and attentions to me? I liked him because he disliked Darcy and was rude enough to tell me in our first real conversation.

I see now the impropriety of his disclosures.

With shame, I realize that I have been little better than Georgiana, deceived by a charming rogue.

I have often prided myself on my powers of observation and judgment, but today I see that I am a fool.

Darcy says, "I trust that you will not disclose these facts, particularly those regarding my sister."

"No, of course not," I promise. "And I am sorry I doubted you. I should not have believed Wickham's lies so readily."

"No," he says, taking my hand in his. "Detection could not be in your power and suspicion certainly not in your inclination. I think we can both agree that Wickham plays the gentleman to perfection, whereas I am often cool and distant." He smiles wryly. "I do not have the talent others have of conversing easily with those I have just met. I cannot catch their tone of conversation or appear interested in their concerns, as I often see done."

His words condemn me. Have I misjudged a reserved man, misreading his silence as arrogance and pride? "Well," I say carefully. "You might not converse easily, but you have made great strides tonight with me."

He looks at me deeply. "But that is because I care about your opinion."

Good heavens. Whatever can he mean?

For a moment, it feels as if we are the only two people in the room and I catch my breath. But then, the noise of the room returns and I pull my hand from his grasp. I see Jane approaching us and I rise to my feet. "If you will excuse me, sir. Thank you for the dance."

7

TUESDAY, EVENING

ELIZABETH BENNET

Jane takes both my hands in hers. "Oh Lizzy," she says breathlessly. "I must speak to you, right away."

Darcy bows. "Then I will retreat and let you have my place," he says.

I watch as he walks away, back into the crowd.

Jane sits down and pats the chair next to her. "Do sit," she urges.

I sit and she says, "I am so happy. I can scarcely breathe, I am so happy." She places a hand over her heart. "I do not deserve it."

For a moment, Jane reminds me of our mother with her heart palpitations. "Deserve what?" I prompt.

"Mr. Bingley."

My eyes widen and I look around to make

certain that we are alone, not to be overheard. "Has he proposed?"

"Yes, and he says he will talk to Father in the morning. Oh, Lizzy, I don't know how I will bear so much happiness! When I think of all the pleasure this will give to our entire family. Our mother will be so pleased. I wish I could tell her now, but I will wait until Father agrees."

I have been happy for Jane, enjoying her joy, but this last statement checks my congratulations. "Are you marrying him for his money? To make our parents happy?"

"No, of course not. Do you think me so mercenary? I would love him no matter his fortune. He is so sensible, so good humoured, so kind."

I believe Jane's sincerity and think that Bingley is a good match for her, but I would never deny the advantages of a steady income. "I am very happy for you," I say finally. "Although I will miss you terribly."

"You must visit Netherfield every day."

I smile. "I can see that I will get my exercise."

"Oh no," she says and laughs a little. "I will send a carriage."

MR. COLLINS

After dancing with Elizabeth, I go to compliment Mr. Bingley and Miss Bingley on the elegance of their entertainment and the hospitality and politeness which marks their behaviour. Mr. Bingley informs me that there will be a light supper at midnight, followed by some music performances, and the evening will end with fireworks. "That sounds delightful. To my knowledge, my patroness Lady Catherine de Bourgh has never had fireworks at her home, Rosings Park, but I believe she would not disapprove, as long as the safety requirements are met."

Mr. Bingley assures me that he has hired Signore Invetto, a man with years of experience.

"An Italian?" I wonder at the wisdom of that.

Miss Bingley asks if I have eaten any of the refreshments. "No, ma'am, I have not availed myself of that pleasure."

"Then I encourage you to do so," she says. "Right away."

"You are all kindness," I tell her and hasten to accommodate her wishes.

At the food tables, I take one of everything and pile it on a little plate. Then I sit down on one of the side chairs and make my way through it methodically. As I am eating my third pastry, fig this time, I overhear Cousin Lydia laugh as she is dancing. I turn in her direction to see her dancing with an officer.

I am momentarily captivated by the joy on her

face. She is young, but there is an energy, a vivacity to her movements that is enchanting.

I decide that that when this dance is over, I will ask her for the next. I think I should dance with each of my cousins, out of politeness if nothing more. I don't think Cousin Elizabeth will mind.

LYDIA BENNET

I danced with an officer, making certain I laughed and flirted with him whenever I was near Darcy to make him jealous, but I don't think he noticed me at all. He was too busy talking with Lizzy, although what they could have to talk about, I don't know.

While I am considering what else I can do to make him notice me, Mr. Collins approaches. "Cousin Lydia, would you please do me the honor of dancing with me for the next set?"

I cringe. Dancing with Mr. Collins would be unbearable. I saw what he did to Lizzy. He has two left feet and no sense of rhythm. "No, I cannot," I tell him. "I have a terrible headache and must sit out for a while."

"You poor, darling girl," he says, leaning forward. "Let me care for you. I can wet my handkerchief and soothe your brow."

"Yes, that is an excellent idea," I say quickly. "Go speak to Miss Bingley and see if she has ice."

"I will," he says. "Right away. I am yours to command."

As he hurries off to find Miss Bingley, I hurry off in the opposite direction. I will have to hide in the card room to avoid him.

FITZWILLIAM DARCY

After dancing with Elizabeth, I speak with Bingley at the refreshment tables. "I have done it!" he says. "I have proposed to Jane Bennet."

That must be why Jane wished to speak with her sister.

I look at Bingley. He is besotted, so there is no dissuading him. I watch as he wolfs down one pastry, then another. "These are delicious," he says and licks his fingers. "Don't you want one, Darcy?"

"No, thank you." I prefer savory rather than sweet treats. Bingley surveys the room. He says suddenly, "Who is the young woman in green standing by herself?"

"If I am not mistaken, I think it is Elizabeth Bennet's friend, Miss Lucas."

"Charlotte Lucas?" Bingley says. "I never noticed before what a fine figure she has."

I am surprised by the change in conversation, but

then again, Bingley when happy can be mercurial. I look at Miss Lucas more critically. I suppose that men can differ in their judgements, but Miss Lucas does not look any better than she did before. Personally, I prefer Elizabeth's figure, which is light and pleasing. Elizabeth also has an excellent bosom in comparison to Miss Lucas.

"Her ankles aren't bad," I say.

"I will ask her to dance," Bingley says. "It is my duty as host to make certain everyone dances."

MRS. BENNET

I glance about the ballroom. Jane is a triumph, as I knew she would be. Bingley has already danced with her twice and continued to talk with her afterwards. Kitty has also danced every dance. I don't know where Lydia is. Mary, of course is sitting to one side of the room with the old maids and matrons. Sometimes I wonder if she is a changeling. How could I have given birth to such a plain child? And Elizabeth danced with Mr. Darcy, which is surprising. I thought him too proud to dance with her. But where is she now? Ah, sitting with Jane. How lovely they look, seated together – one daughter with fair hair and the other with dark.

I look about to see Mr. Bennet, but I cannot find

him, either. If I know him, he has wandered off to a quiet room to find a book and read.

I walk over to the food tables to admire the refreshments. It is an amazing spread with so many sweets. I sip a glass of punch and pop a cooked mushroom into my mouth. The pastries look delicious, but unfortunately, my ballgown is a little tight, particularly in the sleeves, and I know Mr. Bennet will not allow me to buy another, larger gown any time soon. Not when I have already overspent this quarter's allowance.

Mr. Bennet is so strict.

But I suppose it is better for me to avoid sweets and to slim down. I have gotten fat in my old age. Perhaps that is why Mr. Bennet never compliments me.

I sigh. When we were young, Mr. Bennet complimented me all the time. It is so hard to be a beauty and then to grow old. My only happiness now is to find husbands for my daughters. I glance once more at Jane. I do not envy her beauty, for when I was young, I was almost her equal.

After a few minutes, one of the officers joins me at the table. It is Mr. Denny, one of Lydia's favourites. He is slimmer than I like in a young man and has long side whiskers, but the redcoat is flattering. He eats a pastry.

"Is it good?" I ask, wishing I could eat one as well.

He looks over at me and smiles. "Yes. Very good. Do you want one?"

"No, thank you."

He says suddenly, "May I have this dance?"

"Oh, no." I laugh, startled by the question. "I am much too old for you. Wouldn't you rather dance with one of my daughters?" I look for Lydia or Kitty.

Jane is now dancing with someone who is not Bingley. Kitty and Lydia are both dancing now. I cannot find Lizzy, so that leaves only Mary.

I try to guide him in her direction, but Mr. Denny says, "No, ma'am. As much as I am certain your daughters would be charming, I must prefer their mother." He holds out his arm to escort me onto the floor.

I blush. It has been years since I have been the object of a young man's attention. I suspect that Denny must be foxed, but his eyes sparkle so charmingly, I accept. "Very well, if you insist," I say. "But I warn you, I am not as spry as Lydia."

His voice lowers. "A wise man prefers experience to naivete."

I giggle. I never expected Mr. Denny to have such a silver tongue. I look around the room, wishing that Mr. Bennet could see me as I step into the centre and take my place for the dance.

MR. BENNET

I do not like Balls. They are noisy, uncomfortable affairs, but I assume the food will be good and I hope to find a few guests who want to play cards.

I eat some veal cake at the food tables, then finish with a fig pastry. Rather good, I think. Not too sweet.

I look around the room to find my wife. I will ask her to speak to Miss Bingley to get the recipe from her cook.

When I find Mrs. Bennet, I see that she is in the middle of the dance floor, dancing with an officer with long side whiskers who is overly attentive. His hand on her waist during a promenade looks inappropriately close.

I feel a wave of possessiveness that I have not felt in twenty years. What is that blackguard doing, flirting with my wife, whispering in her ear?

I march onto the dance floor, stepping in between the couples. "Mrs. Bennet, what is the meaning of this?" I demand.

"Mr. Bennet, please," Mrs. Bennet protests with a sputter. "I am dancing."

"I can see that. Who is this fellow?"

"Mr. Denny," that man says.

"Why are you not dancing with one of my daughters?"

"Because I prefer your wife."

I catch his shoulder to swing him around to face me and I shove both hands against his chest. "Find yourself another partner," I say brusquely. By this time, the other couples in the set have stopped to watch our altercation.

Mr. Denny shoves at me as well. "I shall do no such thing. If you want to dance with your wife, wait your turn."

Mrs. Bennet tugs on my sleeve. "Please, sir," she says. "Do not lose your temper. Consider my poor nerves."

"I will not have this man disrespecting you. He is overly familiar."

Mr. Denny says stiffly, "You are the one who is disrespectful."

At this, I can hold back no longer. I punch the arrogant puppy on the jaw, and he staggers back.

"Oh Mr. Bennet!" Mrs. Bennet cries and then sways on her feet.

She is fainting, but I catch her before she can fall. "My poor darling," I cry.

Mr. Denny says, "I demand satisfaction, sir," but then I see Mr. Darcy at his side, saying, quietly, "Don't be ridiculous. Do not make a scene."

I hold my wife, watching with satisfaction as Mr. Darcy leads the man away.

After a moment, I realize that the musicians have silenced and everyone in the room is staring at me and Mrs. Bennet. "What are you gawking at?" I say defiantly. "Can't a man dance with his own wife?"

Mrs. Bennet's eyelids flutter open. "You want to dance with me?" she asks weakly.

At that moment, she has never been so near and dear to my heart. It is as if all the years of our marriage have magically slipped away and we are both young again. I reach down and kiss her pink lips. "Forever, my darling girl."

8

TUESDAY, EVENING

ELIZABETH BENNET

Good heavens. What is happening on the dance floor? Is that my father, arguing with Mr. Denny? I glance helplessly at Mr. Darcy, seeking his assistance, and he steps forward, guiding Mr. Denny off the dance floor. Together they walk towards the card room.

What a gentleman.

CAROLINE BINGLEY

The ball is a success. Nearly everyone is dancing and I have received so many compliments on the flowers and the fabric draped on the walls, but I am worried. I don't think the love potion is working. I have tried to dose Darcy's food several times, and he has not looked at me twice. He has not even asked me to dance. I am beginning to think that Mrs. Wyatt is a fraud.

I walk over to the food table and see the footman James that I spoke with this morning. He offers me some pastries on a tray. I eat one of the fig pastries, which doesn't taste as good I remember. Perhaps I should speak to Cook in the morning. As I stand there for a moment, looking out on the dance floor, Mr. Collins demands my attention.

"Miss Bingley," he says. "I must speak to you on the most urgent matter. My Cousin Lydia has a headache and she needs ice. Do you have any?"

How kind of him to help his cousin. "Yes, I am sure we have some," I say. "How much do you need?"

"A few slivers to wrap in my handkerchief should be sufficient."

I send James to the kitchen to fetch some. "And hurry," I say sharply. I don't want Mr. Collins to wait.

James smirks. "Yes, ma'am."

My eyes narrow. I don't like James. I will definitely dismiss him in the morning, but I will think of that later. I would much rather speak to Mr. Collins. I step closer to him and look up into his eyes. "Your poor cousin," I say and touch his arm to comfort him. "Has the dancing been too much for her?"

"It may have been," he says. "She often overexerts

herself. It is something that I hope to influence once we are enga– " He catches himself. "But that is not definite yet. I will not speak of it."

I am astonished. Does Mr. Collins intend to marry Lydia Bennet, that vulgar, irreverent girl? That will never do.

At this moment, there is some commotion on the dance floor. I look over and see Mr. Bennet strike one of the officers. Angry words are spoken and then Darcy is there, walking off the dance floor with the officer.

And Mr. Bennet kisses his wife.

I draw my breath in sharply. I am appalled. I have never seen such vulgarity. All the guests are standing about, shocked, staring. If I don't act now, my party will be ruined.

"Mr. Collins, please help me," I say. "Go tell the musicians to start up again and then dance with me. We must show them proper decorum."

Mr. Collins hesitates. "But what of Cousin Lydia's headache?"

"You will get your ice as soon as the dance has finished."

"Very well," he says and walks with me to the dance floor.

Within minutes, Mr. and Mrs. Bennet have retreated, the music has resumed, and Mr. Collins is my dance partner.

He is not as tall as Darcy, but he is nice and solid, with a conciliatory air. I like him. I find that I like him very much. He does not dance well, sometimes stepping wrong, but that is no obstacle. I can hire dance instructors.

As we dance, I begin to weave my web. "Mr. Collins," I say. "You mentioned earlier that Lady Catherine de Bourgh is your patroness. Tell me more about her."

MR. COLLINS

Miss Bingley is an excellent dancer and as we dance, she keeps up a steady stream of pleasant conversation. She asks me when I decided to become a clergyman and tells me that she has great admiration for men of the cloth. "I know that most of them are men of intelligence and skill that could easily make their living at any profession."

"That is true. If I were not a man of the cloth, I could have been a physician or a barrister."

She nods. "I see that in each of your choices, you wanted to do good in the world, to serve your fellow man."

"I do."

She blushes prettily. "Forgive my impertinence, but I hope that when you marry, you will marry a young woman with a sizeable dowry to help you with your charitable endeavors."

I explain that the Bennet girls do not have large dowries.

"No," Miss Bingley says sadly. "That is a pity. Whereas my dowry is twenty thousand pounds."

My eyes grow wide, afraid to even consider what she might be saying.

She continues, "And I have gone to Mrs. Whitmore's School for Young Ladies, so I know all the proper forms of address and if you wish, I could start a school for Lady Catherine's tenants."

By this time, the dance has ended and we are walking back to the side chairs. I lower my voice. "Miss Bingley, forgive my presumption. Are you suggesting that I marry you?"

"Oh, Mr. Collins," she says with a trill of light laughter. "I would never presume to propose to such a principled man as yourself. That would not be proper. My only suggestion to you is that you follow your heart." At this, she takes my gloved hand and presses it over her left breast. "My heart aches for you, Mr. Collins."

At this moment, I am faced with a dilemma – to either follow my own heart and propose to Lydia Bennet or to accept Miss Bingley's blatant encouragement.

What would Lady Catherine advise?

I believe that she would prefer Miss Bingley, who is more even tempered and better behaved than Lydia, who can be wild. Lady Catherine advised me to marry a girl, not brought up too high, and Miss Bingley's grandfather's fortune was made in Trade.

Indeed, I cannot imagine anyone more suitable to becoming a clergyman's wife. She has already been mistress of Netherfield. She will have no problems running my dear little cottage.

And when I inherit Longbourn, we will be neighbours to her brother. It all seems so tidy.

And as for love, I can learn to love her.

I lower my voice to a whisper so we will not be overheard. "My dear Miss Bingley, will you do me the great honour of accepting my hand in marriage?"

9

TUESDAY, EVENING

CHARLES BINGLEY

Charlotte Lucas is an intelligent young woman who reads much more than I do. She is a fine dancer and when our dance is over, I ask her if she will be my partner at the midnight supper. She is surprised but agrees.

She then excuses herself and I watch as she walks away. She is a lovely girl with intelligent, pleasant parents.

Caroline approaches me. She is walking next to Mr. Collins, holding his hand in hers. "Charles," she says happily. "Wish me well. I am engaged."

"What?"

Mr. Collins interrupts. "In her happiness, your sister speaks too soon. I know that it is proper for me to obtain your permission first. And in order for you to understand my worthiness for her hand, I will outline my reasons for marrying. First, I think it a right thing for every clergyman to set the example of matrimony in his parish. Secondly, I am convinced that it will add very greatly to my happi –"

"Not now," I tell him and fortunately he silences. I turn to my sister. "You want this – this –" I cannot think of a term that is not impolite. "man?"

"I want him more than anything I have ever wanted in my life."

"You love him?"

"Most passionately."

Passionately? That does not sound like my sister. I frown at Mr. Collins who says quickly, "Rest assured, sir. Nothing untoward has happened this evening. I hold your sister in the highest esteem and I would never take any improper liberties until we are safely married before God. Except at that time, once we are married, those liberties will not be improper, as you know. They will be sanctioned by God. Indeed, the wedding ceremony itself reminds us that marriage was ordained for a remedy against sin, and to avoid fornication, such that persons as have not the gift of continency might marry and keep themselves undefiled members of Christ's body."

I struggle to keep my composure. The last thing I

want to hear from a potential brother-in-law is a lecture about liberties and the purposes of the marriage bed. "If you will excuse me, sir," I tell him. "I must speak to my sister privately, first."

"Yes, as you wish," Mr. Collins says, bowing and scraping.

I take Caroline by the hand and lead her out of the ballroom and into one of the sitting rooms. I hastily light a candelabra so we can see each other clearly. "What nonsense is this?" I demand once the door is shut and we are alone. "You want to marry Mr. Collins?"

"I do."

"Are you mad?" To me, Mr. Collins is a prosy bore.

"I don't think so."

I look at her carefully. "How many glasses of punch have you drunk?"

"Only two. I am not inebriated."

"But what about Darcy? You have been chasing him for years."

"I know," she says. "And he does not want to be caught. Tonight I realized that I wanted someone better, someone with a purpose in life."

I do not think for one minute that Mr. Collins is in any way better than Darcy, but I also know that Darcy has never wanted to marry Caroline. Perhaps this is for the best. And to be honest, Mr. Collins is no worse than Mr. Hurst, Louisa's husband. "Are you certain?"

"Yes, I am certain," Caroline says. "And I want you to announce our engagement tonight."

"Why so soon?"

"Because Mrs. Bennet wants him for one of her own daughters, and I don't trust her not to try some stratagem. But once we are formally engaged, there is nothing she can do to stop us."

MARY BENNET

The music is drawing to a close, and once again, no one has asked me to dance. I walk over to the refreshment tables by myself. The fig pastry tastes nasty, but I finish it out of politeness. The punch is fine. I see one of the soldiers sitting in a shadowy corner with his head in his hands. I don't know if he is foxed or dejected.

I walk over up and sit next to him. It is Mr. Denny, who often speaks with Lydia and Kitty. He is a friend of Mr. Wickham. I have seen Mr. Denny half a dozen times in the past few months, but I know nothing of him beyond Lydia's stories. "Are you all right?" I ask.

He groans. "No."

"Too much wine?" I guess.

"No, I have made a fool of myself."

"Why do you say that?"

He shakes his head. "Did you not see me fight with your father?"

"Yes, but he was the fool, not you. I thought you handled yourself well, considering the situation. I don't know what madness possessed my father. He is normally not a jealous man."

"I don't know what possessed me, either." Mr. Denny says. "My behavior was not fitting as an officer and a gentleman."

I place my hand on his arm. "I think you make too much of it. It will be forgotten in a week or two, replaced by some other story."

He looks at me closely. "You are very kind. Your name is Mary, right?"

"Yes."

He smiles. "In this light, you look remarkably like your mother."

He means it as a compliment. It is lovely to be appreciated. I ask him, "Are you already promised for the supper?

JAMES PUCK

I stand by the food tables, rocking back slightly on my feet. My gloved hands are clasped in front of me. There is only one of the tainted fig pastries left. I protect it jealously, wanting to make certain it goes to the most amusing recipient. Already Miss Bingley has fallen in love with the fat clergyman. Serves her right. That was the best complication of the evening, although Miss Elizabeth's father was amusing too. Gentleman Jackson would be proud of that right facer he gave the soldier.

As I survey the guests, I decide that Miss King will be the final recipient. All the servants know that she recently inherited ten thousand pounds. It is a tidy sum, which could fund my snuff shop, if I play my cards right. I weave through the crowd to find Miss King. She is a thin young woman with bony arms, red hair, freckles, and an ill-fitting gown. But right now, she is the most interesting of all Mr. Bingley's guests.

"Pardon me, miss," I say and present the tray containing the last fig pastry with a flourish. "This is from Mr. Bingley with his complements. Sweets to the sweet."

Miss King is no fool. She glances briefly at Bingley who is speaking with his guests across the room, then eats the pastry.

"Excuse me, miss," I say, commanding her attention.

She looks deeply into my eyes. "Yes?"

ELIZABETH BENNET

It is time for the supper and I search out for Mr. Darcy to thank him for helping my father. But when I do find him, Lydia is tugging on the sleeve of his coat. "You shall escort me into supper," she says. "I insist."

At first, I think that this is one of Lydia's jokes, but she appears to be in earnest. Darcy says, "Pardon me, but I have no intention –"

I intervene. "I am sorry, Lydia," I say as I approach them both. "But Mr. Darcy is my partner. He asked to sit with me earlier."

Darcy looks relieved. "Thank you."

Lydia pouts. "How can you be so greedy, Lizzy? First Wickham and now Mr. Darcy. Do you think all the gentlemen should belong to you?"

There is no suitable answer to that question, so I remain silent.

Lydia then turns on Darcy. "I don't think I like you, after all," she says hotly. "You are too high in the instep and not any fun at all!" She flounces away, promising to find someone much better.

Once she is gone, Darcy says, "As much as I appreciate your offer, you do not need to honor it now that your sister has abandoned me. Besides, I have no intention of eating this evening."

I say, "Mr. Darcy, you must do as you prefer, but I did want to thank you for your help with my father earlier."

"It was nothing, I assure you."

"Well, it was not nothing to me. I appreciated it."

His eyes are dark as they look at me. "I am happy to be of assistance in any way."

We stand there for a moment in awkward silence. I ask, "Is Mr. Denny all right, do you think?"

"Yes. His jaw is bruised, but not broken."

"I am glad."

Many of the guests are making their way over to one side of the ballroom where long tables are set up for the supper. Since this is not a formal dinner, some of the guests go singly, others in pairs. I see my parents walk together, looking at each other as if they are newlyweds.

Mr. Darcy bows in farewell. "Good evening, Miss Bennet."

"Mr. Darcy," I say in reply and curtsey. I can't help but consider what he must think of my family – with Lydia's rudeness and my parents' absurdity. No wonder he wants little to do with me.

As I watch him walk away, I am disconcerted by a sense of loss. But this is nonsense. Why should I care what he thinks of me or my family? I have disliked Mr. Darcy for weeks.

But then I realize that my perceptions of him have changed. Mr. Darcy is not the man I thought he was. I suspect that he is infinitely better.

10

WEDNESDAY, EARLY MORNING

FITZWILLIAM DARCY

After the all the abhorrent food I have tasted today, I prefer not to eat supper. I stand back from the crowd and watch as Elizabeth sits at one of the tables across from her parents. Mr. and Mrs. Bennet are holding hands and smiling at each other. Until tonight, I considered Mr. Bennet to be a scholar, not a lover, but his passionate response to his wife is as encouraging as it is amusing. It gives me hope that in my older years, I might be equally in love with my own wife.

But the question that fills my thoughts is the identity of that wife.

I know what my family and friends would want for me – some idealized young woman, someone educated like Caroline Bingley, preferably an heiress with high born connections.

But just as I have never wished to marry Caroline Bingley, I have never met a young woman in London who has stirred my heart and soul like Elizabeth Bennet.

I have spent the last five years, since my father's death, looking for the perfect woman, only to find myself conquered by the gloriously imperfect Elizabeth Bennet.

Bingley stands before the crowd. "Before we begin the supper, I have an announcement to make."

Elizabeth looks sharply at her sister Jane who shakes her head slightly.

"It is my great pleasure to announce the engagement of my sister Caroline Bingley to Mr. Walter Collins."

At this, Mrs. Bennet, who had been smiling at her husband, shrieks. "But that is impossible!" she sputters. "Mr. Collins wants to marry our Lizzy!"

Mr. Bennet shushes his wife. "Come dearest," he says. "Let the young people decide their own lives."

I decide that I might like Mr. Bennet as a father-in-law.

Bingley chooses to ignore the outburst. He continues. "I give you a toast for the happy couple: May your journey to the altar be quick and without mishap. To the happy couple!"

All the guests, except for Mrs. Bennet, raise their glasses.

ELIZABETH BENNET

I cannot believe it. Miss Bingley and Mr. Collins? But they both look happy, and inside my heart, I wish both these irritating people well, even if my rational mind says that they will never be happy together.

As we all eat our cold ham and chicken, my mother engages Lady Lucas in conversation. "If Mr. Collins is not to marry Lizzy, at least Jane still has Mr. Bingley. He is such a charming young man and so rich! And to think of his living only three miles from Longbourn." She smiles at Lady Lucas. "I hope one day your dear Charlotte will be equally fortunate."

"I think she may already be as fortunate," Lady Lucas says slyly and nods her head towards Mr. Bingley at the head of the table. "Perhaps even more fortunate than your Jane."

Along with my mother, I look in Mr. Bingley's direction. He sits by Jane, as I expected, but he also sits by Charlotte Lucas, and he is cutting up pieces of meat and feeding them to her, as if she is a baby bird. Charlotte does not look as if she is enjoying his attentions, but she too polite to refuse them.

Bingley has turned his back toward Jane and is ignoring her.

From the pained expression in Jane's eyes, I can tell that Jane is confused and mortified, but she is too proud to let anyone know. She eats her meal slowly, her face pale.

I excuse myself to go over to Jane. As I stand up, I can hear my mother screech again and my father try to console her. "That conniving tart!" my mother says. "How dare she try to take Mr. Bingley away from Jane?"

Lady Lucas retorts, "All is fair in love and war until there is a ring on her finger."

I walk quickly to Jane. "Excuse me," I say. "May I speak to you privately?"

Jane excuses herself and Mr. Bingley does not even bother to look at her. Together we walk away from the table and through glass doors to the gardens outside. "Oh Lizzy," Jane says once we are away from the other guests. "I don't know what to think."

At that moment, I hate Mr. Bingley. How dare he break my sister's heart?

Jane asks, "Do you think I have offended him somehow?"

"Impossible."

"Or perhaps he talks with Charlotte to hide his feelings for me?"

"Hide his feelings from whom?" I demand. "It makes no sense. Just a few short hours ago he asked you to marry him, and now-" I point back to the ballroom, "this. It is unconscionable. Unforgiveable."

"I am certain there must be a reason," Jane says.

Jane is too kind, but I will have none of it. "No," I say fiercely. "You must not let him treat you poorly."

Jane dabs her eyes with a handkerchief. "No more," she says. "Please. I don't want to cry."

"Very well, we can make plans to torture him tomorrow."

Jane's eyes widen.

"I am joking," I assure her. But at that moment, I do feel like challenging him to a duel. Mr. Bingley who seemed so good and kind, seems like a different person now – like one of the twins in Shakespeare's Comedy of Errors.

We walk together along the lawn until Jane feels composed enough to return to the ballroom. As we enter, we see Mary playing the pianoforte for the entire company. But surprisingly, Mr. Denny is turning the pages of her sheet music for her, as well as accompanying her with a fine baritone voice. The strength of Mr. Denny's voice masks the weaknesses in Mary's.

"I did not know he could sing, did you?" I ask.

Jane says, "It just proves that perhaps we all have hidden talents."

I squeeze her hand. "And your talent is to see the good in everyone."

CHARLES BINGLEY

I open the glass doors that open out from the ballroom to the lawn. "Come everyone," I call. "It is now time for the fireworks." Some of my guests choose to stay indoors and avoid the wet grass, but many come out with me onto the gardens.

As I step outside onto the lawn, I breathe in the cool night air and it seems to clear my mind. I see Jane Bennet sitting on a stone bench along one of the garden paths and I am struck by her beauty.

Suddenly I remember that I am engaged to Jane. I love her.

But I am confused. Why was I enamored by Charlotte Lucas this evening? She is a fine young woman, but she is not Jane.

I motion for the musicians inside the house to play a rousing melody, and then I walk over to Jane. "If you will come with me, I can show you the best place to stand to see the performance."

Jane shakes her head. "I think not."

"Why not?"

She speaks quietly so as not to be overheard. "I love you, Mr. Bingley and tonight I agreed to marry you. But if you cannot be constant, perhaps it would be best if our understanding ends now."

Her words sting, and I know I deserve them. I have been a fool. I take her hands in mine and kiss them. "But I love you. I don't know why I acted so strangely tonight, but I am sorry for it and I beg your forgiveness."

Jane looks at me. "I think it would be best if we discuss this at another time," she says coolly. "Your guests are waiting for the fireworks."

She is correct, although at this moment, I care nothing for my guests or the fireworks. I care only for her.

She says, "Excuse me, Mr. Bingley. I will speak to you another time." And then she leaves me, walking back to the house, her shoulders back, her head held high. She walks like royalty.

I want to run after her, but I sense that any further apologies at this time would be futile.

Through my foolish behavior, I am losing the only woman I have ever truly loved.

One of the footmen who has been assisting Signore Invetto approaches me. "Are you ready to begin the display?"

"Yes."

FITZWILLIAM DARCY

I stand with others in the ballroom, watching the fireworks. The night sky is brilliant with a shower of white as a firework goes up like a rocket and then explodes, creating a huge circle and shower of lights that sprinkles down like magical rain.

"Mr. Darcy!"

I flinch, fearing at first that it is Lydia Bennet returning to bother me, but when I turn I see that it is Elizabeth and my heart leaps. I am pleased that she sought me out.

I bow low to her. "Miss Bennet."

She looks at me earnestly. "Sir, I have a request that may at first seem inappropriate."

Immediately my mind leaps to every delightful inappropriate request she could make. Belatedly, I realize that Elizabeth is still speaking, "I beg your indulgence and for you to answer me honestly," she says.

"I will do my best."

She says. "But first, let us go out into the garden. I do not want to be overheard."

This sounds even better. I follow her out into the cool night air. Rather than stand by the crowd on the center of the lawn, we walk over to one side where there are stone paths and ornamental bushes. The lanterns and moonlight provide some illumination. As we walk, we pass another couple who are hiding in the shadows, kissing.

It is Mrs. Cole and a soldier who is half her age. When discovered, she giggles and they hurry down a path into further darkness.

"Good heavens," Elizabeth says, shaking her head. "I believe the world is going mad tonight."

I agree that there have certainly been some surprises this evening. I motion towards a stone bench and we sit, side by side, turning to face each other.

"Yes. My father punching Mr. Denny and then kissing my mother. Believe me, sir," she says. "My family's behaviour is often embarrassing, but never to the extent on display tonight."

"Do not concern yourself," I say and take her hand in mine. "I believe people will talk more about Miss Bingley's engagement."

"Yes, that was shocking as well. But welcome," she adds quickly. "At least to me. I have worried for the past two weeks that Mr. Collins would propose to me." She shudders at the thought and I give a short laugh, pleased that she never liked her cousin.

I add, "And I feel a sense of relief as well."

She smiles. "Yes, Miss Bingley's pursuit of you has been painfully obvious. But then, you must be accustomed to that." She looks up at me, her eyes bright with amusement. "I assume you are one of the prime catches in the Marriage Market."

I don't want to talk about myself. I say, "Enough of that. Tell me what has upset you."

At my words, her countenance falls. "Yes. This is important. Your friend, Mr. Bingley seems to be acting irrationally. For weeks he has appeared to favor my sister Jane, and for the first few hours tonight, he would not leave her side. But now, it appears that he has shifted his attentions to Miss Lucas."

I nod, for I had noticed that myself. I also thought his behavior at dinner was odd, particularly after his proposal to Jane.

Elizabeth adds, "Now, if he has truly had a change of heart, perhaps it is best that it is apparent now, before Jane fully commits herself to him. But I want to know, for you are his friend – if Bingley is normally so fickle."

As much as it pains me, I must be completely honest with her. "I have seen him in love before, and it often does not last long."

"I see," she says and stares out across the sky at the exploding fireworks. "Has he become engaged before and cried off?"

"No, not that I know of. And in his defense, he seems more taken with your sister than any other woman before her."

"But you saw him at dinner, hanging on Charlotte Lucas's every word?"

"Yes."

She is quiet for a moment, then says, "I wonder if perhaps the punch is too strong. I have never seen so many people behave so out of character from their natures. Mr. Bingley seems to be a man of honour and my father is not a violent man."

"And I suppose Mrs. Cole is usually a pattern card of virtue?"

She nods. "There seems to be some kind of madness in the air."

It is madness how I feel for her. "I believe you are right. But if so, what can be done about it? Should we not succumb as well?"

She looks at me, startled. "What do you mean?"

Her lips are only a few inches from mine. I lean forward and kiss her. She gasps. "Mr. Darcy!" but she does not shrink back, so I kiss her again, this time pulling her against me.

11

WEDNESDAY, EARLY MORNING

ELIZABETH BENNET

I am oddly breathless when we separate. "Mr. Darcy!" I say again, not knowing what else to say. Propriety says that I should react, possibly slap his face for accosting me, but I do not want to strike him. To be honest, my heart is racing and I want to kiss him again, even though I know it is madness.

I never thought my first kiss would be from Mr. Darcy, of all men.

He smiles down at me and my heart flutters. Why did I never realize how beautifully handsome he was before? "Darling Elizabeth," he says and his fingers are soft on my cheek. "You must allow me to tell you how ardently I admire and love you. Marry me and make me the happiest of men."

Marry?

He leans forward to kiss me a third time, but sanity returns and I press my hands against his firm chest. "No, sir," I say quickly and scramble out of his embrace and onto my feet. "Not now, not tonight with all this confusion." I motion to the fireworks above us. "If you must speak to me of love, speak to me tomorrow in the calm light of day. And if you do not renew your suit, I will consider you to be like Bingley or Mrs. Cole."

He starts to protest, but I shake my hands at him to keep him at bay.

"Until tomorrow," he promises. "Or do you mean today since it is already past midnight?"

"Good night, Mr. Darcy," I say firmly and turn to run back to the house.

FITZWILLIAM DARCY

I watch my beloved Elizabeth return to the main house, but I am not discouraged. She would not kiss me as she did if she not care for me. I relive the moment, amazed by my audacity, and yet my heart is calm. I have no more doubts. I have crossed the Rubicon and there is no turning back. Tomorrow I will call on Elizabeth to propose properly and I will speak to her father.

I think a special license will be best, for I do not want to wait for the posting of the banns.

Elizabeth Darcy, how well that sounds.

I think Georgiana will like her, and I hope they will become good friends.

I watch as the fireworks display ends and the guests return to the ballroom. Servants bring their cloaks and capes and eventually everyone prepares to leave. I watch the Bennets especially, thinking that I will soon be a son-in-law to Mr. and Mrs. Bennet. After tonight's adventures, that prospect is not so terrible. They are the last of the company to leave.

I try to catch Elizabeth's eye before she goes. She looks at me briefly, blushes, and turns away to speak to Jane.

Bingley makes a point of thanking the Bennets for coming, and Mrs. Bennet invites him to join them for a family dinner. "You don't need to stand on ceremony with us. You may come at any time."

Bingley says, "I intended to go to Town tomorrow, but now I don't know what my plans are. But I will definitely take you up on your offer as soon as possible." He looks pleadingly at Jane, but she does not smile in response.

Miss Bingley holds Mr. Collin's hand as if not wanting to let it go. "Parting is such sweet sorrow," she says.

"That I shall say good night til it be morrow," Mr. Collins finishes the phrase for her and kisses her hand with a dramatic flourish.

I am embarrassed for them both.

Mrs. Bennet has a militant expression on her face and says, "I think it best if we leave immediately. Come, Mr. Collins. Mr. Bennet."

Once they are gone, Miss Bingley sighs. "What a wonderful evening. To think that I started today a single woman and now I am engaged."

Mrs. Hurst yawns behind her hand and asks when she plans to marry.

"As soon as possible," Miss Bingley says. "I long to set up my own household and meet Lady Catherine de Bourgh."

I refrain from commenting. Lady Catherine is my aunt, one of my least favorite relations. I wonder what she will make of Miss Bingley.

Bingley says, "You can make plans later, but now we should all go to bed. The servants can clean in the morning.

"Do you wish to talk with me?" I ask Bingley for we often drink a glass of port after the women have retired.

"No," he says. "For I will not be fit company tonight."

I nod. "Good night then." I will not miss our talk for I do not want to hear him agonizing over Jane Bennet. If he has lost her affection, he deserves to. He was a fool to flirt so shamelessly with Charlotte Lucas.

MARY BENNET

Everyone is remarkably quiet on the ride back to Longbourn, even Mr. Collins who sits across from me, smiling happily, no doubt congratulating himself on becoming engaged to Miss Bingley with her twenty thousand pounds.

It is so strange. My parents chose to ride home together in the curricle, something they never do.

Jane appears sad and stares out at the dark landscape. Lizzy looks down at her hands. Lydia declares the evening to have been a complete bore. "I wish I had never asked Mr. Bingley to give this ball. Without Mr. Wickham, it was not worth the time or effort."

Kitty says, "I danced every dance," but no one comments.

I did not dance any dance, but Mr. Denny was most attentive, singing with me at the pianoforte and standing beside me when the fireworks went off.

And best of all, when the party ended, he asked, "May I call on you tomorrow, Miss Mary?"

I don't think he meant anything more than a pleasantry, and I don't expect him to seek me out again, but I will treasure this evening for the rest of my life.

12

WEDNESDAY, MID-MORNING

ELIZABETH BENNET

Breakfast is a cheerful affair. I have rarely seen my mother so happy. She wears her favourite day dress and her best lace cap. She glows with good will, even for Mr. Collins who fills his plate with kippers and eggs. "I will admit I was disappointed last night, Mr. Collins," she tells him. "For I thought you preferred Lizzy, but Mr. Bennet says you should marry for love and I agree."

My father smiles at her across the table, and she smiles back at him.

Then she continues, "And he never wanted you for a son-in-law anyway, so I suppose it is all for the best."

My father coughs to hide a laugh.

My mother ends with, "Lizzy will have to marry someone else."

Mr. Darcy? I think, but do not say it. I have not even told Jane about his proposal, for it would not be kind when she is suffering from Bingley's actions. Besides, I am still in a turmoil, not certain what my response should be.

Do I love Mr. Darcy? Could I love him?

Was my prior righteous anger merely a ruse to mask a wounded heart?

I am confused because I now know that Darcy is not the villain Wickham painted, and I have seen that he has a tender side.

Mr. Collins tells me, "Dear Cousin Elizabeth, I humbly beg your pardon if I have in any way given you expectations that I am now unable to fulfill."

"Unless you plan to become a bigamist," my father mutters.

"I beg your pardon?" Mr. Collins asks.

"Nothing," my father says in a good-natured manner with a wave of his hand. "Proceed with your apology. I will not interrupt again."

Mr. Collins continues with his apology that lasts through the remainder of breakfast and shifts into his plans to visit Netherfield. "I should call this morning, don't you think?"

"Yes, definitely," my father says. "Stay the day, if you wish."

After breakfast, my father goes to the library and my mother speaks to Mrs. Hill. Mr. Collins leaves for Netherfield, Mary practices the pianoforte, and Lydia and Kitty plan a walk to Meryton. They want to converse with Aunt Phillips about the ball and hopefully to see some of the officers. Lydia hopes that Wickham will be back in town.

"Be careful," I warn her. "I don't think Wickham is as good as he seems."

Lydia snaps, "You have been listening to Mr. Darcy, so you are prejudiced against him."

She is correct. "Forgive me," I say. "I just don't want him to take advantage of you."

"I can take care of myself," she says hotly and ties the ribbons of her bonnet with shaking hands. "Come, Kitty."

They leave in a hurry, leaving me and Jane in the sitting room. Jane takes out some sewing and I join her. "How are you feeling?" I ask gently.

"I feel very foolish," Jane says. "I have built up a romance in my mind that was based on thin air. Mr. Bingley does not love me. He is merely a polite, amiable man."

"If he does not love you, why did he propose?"

"An impulse, perhaps? One that he regretted later?"

I don't know what to say, for I fear she may be

right. "I am so sorry," I say. "And if he doesn't want you, he is the fool."

CAROLINE BINGLEY

My maid opens the curtains to my bedroom and I groan, not wanting to wake. But eventually I open my eyes, squinting at the light. My maid has brought a small tray with pastries and a cup of hot chocolate.

She asks, "What would you like to wear this morning?"

"The orange."

She pulls an orange dress from my closet and drapes it over the foot of the bed. I sit up to watch her work. "I had the strangest dream," I tell her idly, but I do not give her the particulars. I dreamed that I became engaged to Mr. Collins, the Bennets' cousin.

As she chooses shoes and stockings for me, she says, "Mr. Collins has called and is waiting in the sitting room. Your brother is currently with him. Do you wish to join them?"

"What?" I shriek.

She repeats herself and I realize that it was not a dream. I am engaged to Mr. Collins. Suddenly all those memories are not bits of dreams, they are real.

What have I done?"

I tell her to hurry with my dress and to send for

my brother. I need to speak to him privately, before I speak with Mr. Collins.

"Yes, ma'am."

Within fifteen minutes, I am dressed and my hair is pulled back into a bun. Charles comes to my room. "What is all the excitement?"

"Charles, I have made a mistake," I say desperately. "I do not know what I was thinking last night, but I do not wish to marry Mr. Collins."

Charles closes the door behind him. "It is too late, Caroline. We made a public announcement. There is no going back now."

I am astonished. I have never known Charles to be so hard and unyielding.

"Of course there is," I argue. "I can cry off and we will return to London."

"But I am not going back to London. I am going to stay here and make amends to Jane Bennet."

I am trapped. "Surely, you don't want me to marry a man I despise."

"You did not despise him last night. You said you loved him passionately."

I vaguely remember saying that, even feeling that way, but now, my feelings are completely different. If I did not know better, I would think someone had given me a love potion. I hurry to my dresser and remove the bottle from Mrs. Wyatt.

"What's that?" Charles asks.

I hand it to him, with Mrs. Wyatt's note. "It is a love potion. I bought it to give Mr. Darcy, but I think there must have been a mishap. I think someone gave it to me instead."

My brother reads the note and opens the bottle to smell it. "Whew," he says. "If anyone used this against you, Caroline, you would have noticed it. No, this is all nonsense." He sets the bottle down. "There is no such thing as love potions, and I am appalled that you tried to trick Darcy."

"I just wanted him to love me!"

"And now Mr. Collins loves you. I suppose there is some divine justice in that."

"I won't marry him," I say and fold my arms across my chest. "I refuse."

"Fine. But if you don't marry him, you can go live in Yorkshire with Great Aunt Martha, but you will not live with me – neither in London or here at Netherfield."

"You would abandon me?"

"I am tired of your dramatics, Caroline. You have already refused two offers from good men because they weren't Darcy. And now you threaten to jilt Mr. Collins."

I can tell from his tone of voice that he means what he says.

If I don't marry Mr. Collins, I will never go to London again.

Charles says, "It is your choice, Caroline."

I have made my bed and now I must lie in it.

FITZWILLIAM DARCY

I ride over to Longbourn to call on Elizabeth, but as I approach the house, I see that she is in the garden, so rather than knocking on the front door, I dismount and walk around to meet her. She is sitting on a blanket, weeding the vegetable garden. She is wearing a wide brimmed bonnet to shield her face from the sun. "May I join you?" I ask.

"Only if you help," she says.

So I sit beside her and pull some the weeds myself. It is simple work and not too dirty. When I was a child, I loved working in the gardens at Pemberley, but it has been years since I have dug in the dirt. We work in silence for several minutes, and I ask, "Have you thought of our conversation last night?"

She says, "I think of little else."

I wait for her to say more, and eventually she says, "I have a friend who thinks that happiness in marriage is entirely a matter of chance and that it does not matter how much one partner knows about the other, because both will alter so much afterwards, bringing vexation and grief."

"You think that I am going to change into someone you don't like?"

"You might," she says. "And so might I. It happened to my parents."

"They appeared to be simpatico last night."

"Yes, and that was quite surprising. My father has paid no heed to my mother for years. I don't know what made the difference yesterday."

I smile. "My valet says the Netherfield servants suspect a love potion."

"How absurd," Elizabeth says, amused.

"Apparently Miss Bingley recently hired the services of Mrs. Wyatt, who is known for her love potions."

"I believe Miss Bingley capable of buying a love potion, but I can't believe a love potion would be effective."

"Neither can I, but it would explain the strange happenings last night."

Elizabeth is thoughtful. "Like Mr. Bingley and Miss Lucas."

"Yes."

She looks me straight in the eye. "Does it explain your sudden love for me?"

I draw my breath in sharply. "No. I have been falling in love with you almost from the moment I met you. And besides that, I ate nothing at the ball."

She says, "Why do you love me?"

I never expected an interrogation, but I will answer any question to put her mind at ease. "I was first impressed by the liveliness of your mind, and as time went on, I saw your kind heart and your honesty. And gradually I came to realize that I wanted to spend the rest of my life with you."

She considers my words and for a long moment I feel as if my happiness hangs by a precarious thread.

Should I say more? Should I take her in my arms and kiss her again? Her bonnet may make such a move awkward.

Having never been in love before, I fear that my efforts will be inadequate.

Then her fine eyes sparkle with amusement and she says dryly, "Then you are in luck, Mr. Darcy, for I wish to spend the rest of my life with you, too."

At this, I give out a whoop of joy and I do kiss her.

Her bonnet does not survive the onslaught.

EPILOGUE: EIGHT MONTHS LATER

ELIZABETH DARCY

"Dearly beloved, we are gathered together here I in the sight of God, and in the face of this congregation, to join together this Man and this Woman in holy Matrimony; which is an honourable estate, instituted of God..."

The minister continues to speak the familiar words of the ceremony and I glance briefly at Darcy, remembering our wedding eight months before.

Then my gaze returns to my sister Jane and her future husband, Mr. Bingley. Jane is radiant in her happiness, easily the most beautiful bride in the history of Meryton. Mr. Bingley is handsome, too, in a new frock coat. He looks amazed and relieved, as if he thought this day would never come.

EPILOGUE: Eight months later

Poor Mr. Bingley had to prove his constancy before Jane trusted him enough to marry him. She never believed the rumours about love potions. I know my mother thinks that Jane was too hard-hearted not to forgive him quickly, but I think her resistance made Bingley value her good opinion more.

I know that is a factor in the success of my own marriage. As a wealthy man, surrounded by women who flattered him, Darcy was sick of civility, of deference, of officious attention. My impertinence caught his attention. And now, the occasional application of it adds spice to our union. Darcy has learned to laugh at himself and is gradually becoming less imposing in social situations.

As for the love potions, I am not certain what I believe. All I know is that my parents changed for the better. My father's renewed attentions to my mother made her happier and less fretful, which in turn made him like her company better. He is no longer as demonstrative as he was at the Netherfield ball, thank heavens, but he spends less time in his study, and they are happier. And my mother likes knowing that her husband almost challenged a man to a duel. As she often tells her friends with pride, "Mr. Bennet is such a jealous man, he doesn't like me to flirt with anyone."

EPILOGUE: Eight months later

What she does not remind them is that the man who was flirting with her is now her son-in-law. That would be too awkward a story.

But three months after the ball, Mr. Denny proposed to Mary, which surprised us all. Mary has never been an effusive girl, but she appears to be content. Especially now as she stands beside her new husband in the church. I like Mr. Denny, even though I do not like his whiskers. Darcy has teased me, threatening to grow a similar pair of sideburns. I have told him that I would love him even if he grew an entire beard and looked like a bear, but that I prefer him clean-shaven.

Another surprising union was the recent one of Charlotte Lucas and Colonel Forster. He is a pleasant, level-headed man, middle-aged and with grey hair. Not exactly the picture of a romantic hero, but Charlotte is pleased. As she wrote to inform me of their engagement, "I am not romantic like you; I never was. I ask only a comfortable home and considering Colonel Forster's character, connections and situation in life, I am convinced that my chance of happiness with him is as fair, as most people can boast on entering the marriage state."

I wish her well.

As the wedding ceremony continues and the vows are given, Darcy takes my hand, squeezing it

EPILOGUE: Eight months later

gently as if to say that he is thinking of our wedding also.

The wedding breakfast is held at Longbourn, although much of the food is from the Netherfield kitchens. I recognize the pastries and eat an apple one. I notice that Bingley avoids them entirely. Jane says he rarely eats desserts these days.

As I mingle with the guests, I meet with Bingley's sister, Mrs. Collins. She is great with child and rubs a hand over her rounded stomach when she sees me. "Lady Catherine thinks I might be having twins," she informs me with a superior air, as if the timing and quantity of one's offspring is a competition.

"How nice for you," I say politely.

Mrs. Collins looks pointedly at my stomach, which is still flat. "And how is Mr. Darcy? Feeling poorly, is he?"

I realize that this is a veiled criticism implying that my husband, unlike her husband, is incapable of producing an heir. I hold back a laugh. "No, he is in excellent health, thank you."

"I am glad to hear it," she says with a sneer.

I do not tell her, for I have not told anyone except for my husband, that I have missed my courses and that I may have a child by Christmas. At present, it is my secret, my personal joy.

Having seen Darcy with his sister Georgiana, I believe he will be an excellent father.

EPILOGUE: Eight months later

I leave Mrs. Collins to speak to my parents who are conversing with Mrs. Forster. "Oh Lizzy," my mother says as I approach, "The militia is moving to Brighton and your father says we can visit them this summer!"

"Who is to go?"

"All of us," my mother says happily. "Naturally, you and Jane won't, and Mary will be there already. So Kitty and Lydia and I will go. And there will be sea bathing and so many balls and parties. And your father has agreed for new gowns all around."

"Will you go also?" I ask my father.

He puts an arm around my mother's waist. "Of course. Can you imagine Mrs. Bennet in a camp full of soldiers? If I'm not there, some fortune hunter might take off with her."

My mother giggles. "Oh, Mr. Bennet, don't be ridiculous."

Later as Darcy and I walk privately in the garden wilderness outside, I tell him of parents' plans. "Do you think it wise? Kitty and Lydia are still very young, still impressionable and giddy."

He pats my hand that rests on his arm. "Do not fret. They should be fine. Your father will keep an eye on them. And at least we know one villain who won't bother them."

He refers to Wickham who left town and the militia a few weeks after our wedding. According to

EPILOGUE: Eight months later

Denny, Wickham had planned to marry Miss King to pay his debts, but then she ran off to Gretna with one of Bingley's footmen. Gossip says Wickham went to London, but we, thank heavens, have heard nothing more of him.

"I suppose you are right. I should not worry."

We walk for a few more minutes, and Darcy says, "I think Bingley and Jane will be happy."

"So do I." Will Jane be as happy as I? I don't know for happiness is difficult to quantify, and each of are so different. All I know is that Jane only smiles, whereas I laugh.

I look up into the eyes of my dear husband. "There is something about a wedding that makes me sentimental, Mr. Darcy."

He smiles down at me with a familiar warmth. "Excellent. How soon can we leave?"

"Another hour at least," I say. "We will need to say good-bye to Jane and Charles."

Darcy considers that. "And since Georgiana will be in the carriage with us, and then she'll want dinner, that means eight, possibly nine hours before we can be completely private."

"Too long?" I guess. At Pemberley, Darcy often closes doors during the day so he can give me a quick kiss away from the servants' or his sister's gaze.

"Much too long," Darcy says and walks me

EPILOGUE: Eight months later

behind a large oak tree, where we will be out of sight from the house. Darcy leans my back against the rough bark of the tree trunk, but I do not mind. "Prepare to be kissed, Mrs. Darcy."

I laugh.

The End

AUTHOR'S NOTE:

I hope you enjoyed *Darcy's Midsummer Madness.* I have always liked reading Shakespeare and the star-crossed lovers in Midsummer's Night's Dream were the inspiration for this story.

If you liked this book, check out my other Jane Austen Variations:

Stealing Darcy
Bewitching Mr. Darcy.
Frankenstein Darcy
Darcy the Beast

To receive a free download of *Stealing Darcy,*

Author's Note:

please go to my website and sign up for my VIP reader's group. http://cassgrix.com/sd-fd-signup2/

Finally, I love to hear from my readers. You can email me at: cass.grix.author@gmail.com

Or leave a review. I love reviews.

FYI, I have two pen names for Jane Austen Variations. I write more traditional versions under the name Jane Grix and my paranormal versions under the name Cass Grix. I do this because not all readers want paranormal stories – kind of like having mint in your chocolate. If you want to check out my more traditional, but still very fun Jane Grix titles, go to my website (and there are some freebies there, too): janegrix.com.

Thanks.

Happy reading,

Cass

http://cassgrix.com/sd-fd-signup2/

Author's Note:

Website: www.cassgrix.com
Facebook: https://www.facebook.com/Cass-Grix-1271639419512755/
Email: mailto:cass.grix.author@gmail.com

And now, here is a BONUS excerpt from one of my Jane Grix stories, Chapter One of Darcy's Spotless Reputation © 2017

Excerpt from *Darcy's Spotless Reputation* by Jane Grix

Fitzwilliam Darcy was a methodical man, and he believed in the efficacy of habit. He went to bed religiously no later than midnight and woke every morning, no later than six a.m. to a cold bath. He found that the application of cold water was invigorating and he believed that it was one of the reasons for his robust health. His preference was to dip into the pond waters at Pemberley, but when travelling elsewhere, he made do with either a tub of cold water or if that was not available, a pitcher of cold water and a rough cloth.

At present, he was staying in Hertfordshire with his friend Charles Bingley and as fortune would have it, Netherfield had a small pond in the midst of some decorative gardens. Every morning of his visit, Darcy dressed in casual clothes and walked down to the gardens, where he would strip and bathe, then dry off with a towel and dress to return to the house before anyone else was the wiser.

But on this morning, he did not wake naturally before six a.m. He had spent the evening before dining with Bingley and some of the officers in the local militia. Too much wine had been consumed, and he, in a surprising lack of discipline, had slept in. Therefore, his trip to the gardens was much later than he liked. He thought the odds of his being discovered were slim because the November weather was cold and the air damp with mist and a light sprinkling of rain.

The night before it had rained, a torrential downpour that left the ground muddy.

But Darcy was not concerned. His valet Mr. Bowles never complained about muddy boots.

As he walked, Darcy thought about Elizabeth Bennet. She was one of Bingley's neighbours, the second daughter of a gentleman, that he had seen several times in the past three weeks. For some reason he thought of her often, much more than her meagre attractions warranted.

He had seen her first at an Assembly when Bingley tried to get him to dance. He had looked at her without admiration and dismissed her as nothing out of the ordinary. He had scarcely allowed her to be pretty, and in discussing her with his friends, he said she had hardly a good feature in her face, but then his opinion began to change.

He noticed that her countenance was rendered uncommonly intelligent by the beautiful expression of her dark eyes.

He had previously detected more than one failure of perfect symmetry in her form, but upon further observation, he was forced to acknowledge that her figure was light and pleasing.

And her manners which were not those of the fashionable world, were easy and playful.

He was drawn to her. He wished to know more, and recently at a party at Sir William Lucas's, he spoke with her twice. He even asked her to dance, which she declined with an arch look that intrigued him.

As a gentleman of extensive property and an income over ten thousand pounds a year, he was accustomed to young women fawning over him, seeking his attention and approval. But Miss Elizabeth Bennet was different.

The rational part of him thought that her actions were just another attempt to flirt with him, but the emotional part of him wanted to command her attention, with the hope of winning her over.

It was most disconcerting.

Miss Bingley had noticed his obsession for Miss Elizabeth and had teased him, implying that he had fallen in love with her and that Mrs. Bennet would soon be his mother-in-law.

That had been enough to bring him back to his senses. Mrs. Bennet was a vulgar, shrill woman, with one brother a lawyer and the other a merchant. Despite her many charms, Elizabeth Bennet's family and connections made it certain that she could never be Mistress of Pemberley.

He was a fool to even entertain the idea.

And he did not want to marry anyway, at least not for a few more years. There would be ample time in the future to put his neck in the parson's noose.

Darcy walked briskly and soon he was at the edge of the Netherfield pond. Along the bank, there was a cement path and several stone benches.

He stepped out of his boots, stockings, pantaloons and waistcoat. He lined the boots up next to the bench and neatly folded his clothes. Then, wearing only a loose-fitting lawn shirt that reached down past his hips, he stood and performed two minutes of stretching exercises, which included jumping and push-ups.

Then he removed the shirt, folded it as well, and stepped into the cold water as naked as the Good Lord made him.

At Pemberley, he could dive straight in, but here at Netherfield, the water was not as deep. He stepped into the cold water quickly, for he believed that a quick immersion was better than a gradual descent.

"Ah," he gasped at the freezing water. He bent down to swim for several yards, enjoying the harsh sensations. He then immersed himself, diving under the surface so the water covered his head as well. He finally returned to the surface, took a large breath and swam for ten minutes.

When he left the water and walked, dripping, over to the stone bench, he could not see his clothes.

He walked to each of the stone benches, but to his dismay, his clothes had not fallen to the ground. They were nowhere to be found.

And he did not have even a towel for modesty.

"Damnation."

At breakfast, Elizabeth Bennet received a letter from her older sister Jane, informing her that she was ill and currently staying at Netherfield, too sick to travel the three miles home to Longbourn. She had gone to Netherfield the night before to eat dinner with Bingley's two sisters, Miss Bingley and Mrs. Hurst.

Mrs. Bennet was thrilled with the news, for she wanted Jane to stay at Netherfield in order to secure the affections of Mr. Bingley. Mr. Bingley was the most recent addition to their social circle – a pleasant young gentleman rumoured to have an income of four thousand pounds a year. He was currently renting Netherfield Park with his unmarried sister acting as hostess.

"I am so thankful for that rain," Mrs. Bennet said happily. "I knew it was most likely that they would ask her to spend the night, but for her to catch a cold, that was most fortuitous."

Mr. Bennet looked up from his newspaper. "Not if she dies from it."

Mrs. Bennet said, "People do not die of little trifling colds."

Elizabeth glanced at the letter again, narrowing her eyes to read Jane's script. Jane had said that she was very unwell at the beginning of the letter, but by the end she said it was only a sore throat and a headache. No doubt, she did not wish to complain or exaggerate, but knowing Jane, she was worse than she stated. Elizabeth said, "I want to go see her."

"Do you want me to send for the horses?" Mr. Bennet asked.

"No," Elizabeth said. "I know they are needed on the farm. I don't mind the walk." Indeed, there was nothing she liked better than a long walk, outside, by herself. She was the second of five sisters and her home was rarely quiet. Her father found respite by retreating to his study and closing the door. Elizabeth, with no personal study, went walking instead.

Mrs. Bennet said, "In this weather? In all this dirt? You will not be fit to be seen when you get there."

"I shall be fit to see Jane," Elizabeth said.

At that moment, the youngest daughter Lydia interrupted their conversation to repeat some gossip she had heard from Mrs. Phillips, Mrs. Bennet's sister, the day earlier. Mrs. Bennet said, "Do what you want, Lizzy, but don't make a spectacle of yourself."

"Yes, ma'am. I will do my best." Elizabeth had a natural grace to her movements, but sometimes she was awkward, as if not sufficiently noticing her surroundings. If she was not careful, she might bump into the furniture. Mrs. Bennet thought it was because she spent too much time reading – "Your head is in the clouds. Just like your father!" And Elizabeth, in order to compensate for her occasional mishap, had developed a wry sense of self-deprecating humour.

Kitty and Lydia offered to walk with her as far as Meryton, so the three young ladies set off together. Elizabeth wore a heavy pelisse as well as a shawl and sturdy ankle boots.

"If we make haste," Lydia said as they walked

along, "Perhaps we may see something of Captain Carter before he goes."

A local militia was stationed at Meryton and Elizabeth's two younger sisters could talk of little else. They giggled, they simpered, and they planned stratagems to win the hearts of all the officers.

Elizabeth could admire a man in a redcoat, but she was not giddy.

In truth, she had begun to wonder if she would ever marry. Marriage seemed a precarious endeavour. Few of the marriages she had observed were happy ones. Her Aunt Phillips continually complained about her husband's stinginess, Lady Lucas complained that Sir William was forever under her feet, and her mother complained that Mr. Bennet had no compassion for her nerves.

It seemed to Elizabeth that women spent the first years of their lives trying to catch a husband and then spent the remainder of their lives complaining about him.

Granted, Mrs. Bennet was a silly, sometimes hysterical woman, but her father, instead of encouraging her to become more rational, found humour in her weaknesses and sometimes exploited them for his own amusement. And whenever the domestic situation became too chaotic, he hid away in his study.

If Elizabeth ever chose to marry, she hoped her

husband would be more like her Uncle Gardiner – a blunt, cheerful man who adored his wife. The Gardiners had four children and Mrs. Gardiner seemed content.

At Meryton, Elizabeth parted from her sisters. Kitty and Lydia walked off to the lodgings of one of the officer's wives, and Elizabeth continued her walk alone, crossing field after field at a quick pace, jumping over stiles and springing over puddles with impatient activity.

As she neared Netherfield, she admired its decorative gardens. She had often walked to Netherfield when she was a child, so she walked confidently among the tall cone shaped shrubberies and sculpted hedges, her boots making little sound on the gravel walk. She noticed that the rose garden was brown with the plants already cut back for winter, but some of the pale yellow hydrangea were in bloom.

She then turned a corner, heading towards the house and ran straight into a man – a naked man.

She screamed.

~

Darcy's Spotless Reputation by Jane Grix

Made in the USA
San Bernardino, CA
08 June 2020